The Long Road North

QUENTIN SUPER

PAGE PUBLISHING, INC.
New York, NY

First originally published by Page Publishing, Inc. 2017

ISBN 978-1-64027-387-0 (Paperback)
ISBN 978-1-64027-388-7 (Digital)

Printed in the United States of America

CHAPTER ONE

The choice was mine. I could both give up and call it a day, or I could keep fighting and push myself to the next destination. So many times in life, we are presented with options. Usually one of the options is easier. The other is typically harder but more rewarding. On this day, I had the option to take the easy route. I could have just called Bruce and had him pick me up. That would have ended all my misery and allowed me an easier path to the ultimate destination. Yet on this day, there was no room for quitting. I had quit many different ventures in life because I was lazy and didn't want to have to work for anything. I couldn't do that to myself any longer. I looked into the sky then deep into my soul and found the answer. I was going to persevere and keep riding, no matter how hard it was going to be.

I had just moved from Osseo to St. Cloud, two cities in Minnesota that are separated by only forty minutes but are in few ways comparable. My move was precipitated by my desire to complete my bachelor's degree and join the rest of my peers in adulthood. With this transition, I thought my life was taking a turn for the better. Considering that every depiction of college life in film and television is of the partying, sexual nature, I figured that my move from the confines of my parent's home would lead to me having opportunities with women previously seen only in my imagination. This was going to be the time in my life where I was going to break out of my social shell and finally begin to evolve as a stereotypical "bro."

I didn't have any real motivations to go to St. Cloud State University. My best friend at the time went there, so I felt obligated to be where he was. That isn't a bad reason to go to a school, but perhaps it should not have been my deciding factor. Yet this is how I lived my life. I always searched for the easiest possible way to do things. I didn't like going the extra mile because that would require more effort on my part. At the time of my move to St. Cloud, the best way to describe me was a tall, skinny kid with brown hair that was too long and didn't have the necessary style to be considered cool. I had lost my virginity a few months prior, but that still did not give me the confidence necessary to thrive in the college scene.

I moved to St. Cloud in August, right after my mom's annual family golf tournament. I began working a job that started at 4:00 a.m. because I decided I wanted to have my nights off. On my first night away from home, I was watching the Yankees and Red Sox play. It was the game where Alex Rodriguez, coming off a steroids suspension, was mercilessly booed by the Fenway Faithful and plunked with a pitch. He would later go on to hit two home runs in that game. After the game ended, I thought A-Rod was the man. He didn't care what people said or did to him. He simply went out there and did his thing.

School was still a few weeks from starting, so I had time to adjust to my new work schedule and get to know my roommates better. Things were going as expected until I became ill. It was the middle of the summer, so I did not understand why I had such violent flu symptoms. A few days passed and my condition did not become better, so I went home to get an appointment at the doctor's office. I went through a standard physical; meaning I got my blood and heart rate checked. They even smacked my knee with that weird nose-looking instrument. The doctor who evaluated me was a younger woman of Indian descent. She was feeling my stomach to check my body fat, then remarked about how muscular my core felt. "You must work out," she said with a smile. It was a confidence-boosting moment. I got a noticeable erection that I couldn't contain by just thinking about her compliment.

I was later sitting in the waiting room when she approached me. "I'm sorry to have to tell you this, Mr. Super, but I am afraid you have mono." I knew what mono was and what this diagnosis meant. Earlier that summer, I had been seeing someone. I informed her of my recent diagnosis and she said that she also had mono before. I wrongfully assumed that she gave it to me. I told my roommates the news, and they all became paranoid that I would transmit it to them. It was only a few days into my tenure at the house and already I was the social pariah.

One of my roommates was a guy named Kyle "Scooter" Boland. He was an average-sized aviation major from rural Independence, Wisconsin. I have this belief that people from small towns don't see things the way that people from urban societies do. For example, why is running over a turtle with your oversized pickup entertaining? Granted, someone who finds that thrilling might ask me why I feel the need to grow my hair out and pay forty dollars for cologne. To oversimplify, we are all products of our upbringing.

Regardless of our backgrounds, Scooter and I actually got along very well. We would go out and party, and then the next day reminisce and have a few laughs as we tried to process our bloated stomachs and unrelenting headaches.

About a month into the school year, we went to Oktoberfest in La Crosse, Wisconsin. I didn't know what I was getting myself into. I only knew that he and I were going to his preferred area of the Midwest, which at the time was exciting because I thought we would connect on some deeper level.

From the inception, the trip wasn't what I expected it to be. On the drive there, I saw cow pastures, which smelled so bad that I thought about asking him to turn the car around. The first night there, he tried to pawn me off on a woman who everyone considered to be damaged goods. The worst part of the supposed setup was that her mom was following her around everywhere she went.

"Is your mom going to be here all night?" I asked, trying not to show my frustration because I wanted to woo her into sleeping with me.

"Yes. My mom and I go everywhere together!" she said in this party-girl laugh.

Needless to say, I didn't fit in and felt alone at times because he was with his old buddies, and I was relegated to my crappy Samsung smartphone. It wasn't that I didn't have *any* fun. The bars in La Crosse were packed each night, so at the very least I was able to people watch and embrace a new environment. My biggest downfall was that I tried too hard to be someone I wasn't comfortable being, in this case a raging party animal. In doing this, I lost sight of what could have potentially been an enjoyable weekend.

I didn't realize it at the time, but the drive there would end up being the most significant aspect of the trip to La Crosse. We stopped to pick up Scooter's friend, Ryan Brandenburg. Ryan was much like Scooter in that he was an average-built male from the rural part of Wisconsin. The defining feature that set him apart from others was his balding head. It was unfortunate that he was losing his hair at the young age of twenty-one, and that bad luck was enhanced by his friends constantly bashing him for it.

I didn't care that Ryan had a receding hairline. What irritated me about him was that he treated me as an outsider as soon as I met him. What initially set me off was that when we picked him up, he offered everyone in the car a beer except me. To this day, his rationale for this action isn't fully explained. Being denied a beer didn't only make me sober; it made me feel degraded, like an outcast that wasn't welcome in this particular group.

That same night, Ryan tried picking a fight with me at a bar. It wasn't a physical fight. It was more a battle of wits and ideology. I was already not a fan of him because he passed me over in the beer department, and now I could no longer be in his presence. His treatment of me was so bad that I stormed out of the bar and went back to our digs for the night. *Fuck that kid*, I thought. I didn't want to ever see him again.

For the remainder of the weekend, nothing confrontational happened between the two of us. Later that year, Scooter approached me about our living situation for the following school year. At the time we had four people who were committed to living together, but we needed a fifth person for the house we were looking into renting.

"Ryan is thinking about moving up here," he said, my head turning to gauge his seriousness.

I thought I needed to get my hearing checked. I'm a forgiving person, but did Scooter seriously expect me to want to live with him? Scooter knew of our issues in La Crosse, making his inquiry somewhat appalling.

I let the idea fester for some time. After my pondering, I figured that rooming with him would not be the end of my world. Obviously I didn't hold him in high regard, but everyone else really liked the idea of having him around. I realized I could either complain about Ryan moving in, or I could reverse course and learn to tolerate him.

This was part of my maturation process. In the past I would have wrote him off and did everything in my power to ensure that he and I would not cross paths again. The new me, after only a few short months into my St. Cloud tenure, decided that I would likely be unhappy if I never tried to expand out of my comfort zone.

Once I learned Ryan would be moving in with us, I began reaching out to him, trying to make him feel welcome. He came up one weekend when we hosted a party, and we were amicable.

"So how's life back in Wisconsin?" I shyly asked after taking a sip of Angry Orchard.

"It's okay." Some silence ensued. "Do you want a shot of Rumple Minze?" he asked as he too took a swig out of his beer.

Rhino later stepped foot in my room, which for me instantly established us as friends. We had no issues the whole weekend, so things had seemingly turned around. The thing about guys is we try to act like we have all these people we don't like, but the reality is if you put a drink in our hands and force us to be cordial, we will probably get along just fine. That is what happened with Ryan and I that weekend. I got over myself and learned to adjust to something new. He presumably did the same thing. I started to look forward to his arrival in St. Cloud. It was an opportunity to make the most out of my new living situation.

A couple months later, Scooter and I went back to Wisconsin for a wedding. It was an eventful weekend. I got to know some of Scooter's old friends better, and we ended up having an enjoyable time. It was during this weekend that Scooter's friend, Brett, referred to Ryan as Rhino, a nickname that was apropos to his personality. Since then, Ryan became Rhino.

On our first night there, Rhino came out with us. We went to the bars and hung out. It was there that Rhino was first introduced to the new me.

In the less than a year since I moved to St. Cloud, I behaved in ways that I had never imagined. Up until the time I was twenty years old, all I had ever wanted was to lose my virginity. When I was twenty, it finally happened, albeit rather unceremoniously while I was housesitting for my brother. It wasn't an experience I ever look back on with fondness, mostly because I didn't even climax. I was too psyched out by my friend Trevor telling me, "Your first time won't be that good because you will only last about ten seconds." Regrettably, I took that advice to heart and had probably one of the worst first sexual experiences possible.

Eventually, I did have better experiences, including the hallowed orgasm. Like most people, I loved it, but perhaps I loved it too much. In St. Cloud, I started getting sexually involved with a lot of women. Some of them were good people who saw me as more than just an object. Others were as selfish and horny as I was. I met people who I would have liked to continue seeing, and I met people who made me wake up the next morning with regret.

All these encounters happened too quickly. I wasn't mature enough to handle the responsibility that came with being promiscuous. I was in a rut. I didn't think what I was doing was wrong, but it also didn't feel right. I repeatedly told myself, "*This is what college is supposed to be like,*" whether I believed my own thoughts or not. I needed something new to devote my free time to because the path I was traveling would only be filled with loneliness and regret.

CHAPTER TWO

It was now August, three weeks before my senior year was set to begin. That summer had been dragging along. I was taking seven credits as I worked closer towards graduation. There were not many people my age in St. Cloud; keeping busy outside of the classroom was a challenge. Not by choice but more by opportunity and environment, I deferred sleeping around. This actually ended up benefitting me. I began hanging out with a great guy who pleaded with me "to try being friends with women before trying to sleep with them." His words would prove true because I wound up meeting one of my best friends, Miranda.

Miranda was a stunning, model-like woman who was a few years older than me. She attracted attention everywhere we went because of her rocking body and bubbly personality. I was lucky because initially I had not followed my friend's advice. As expected, I tried to have sex with her. Miranda was smart enough to see that I was a dumb young male who thought more often with my genitalia than with any semblance of intellect. Because of her wisdom, we moved past my immature desires and formed an unbreakable bond. We leaned on each other for support, nurturing each other in times of need and embodying characteristics of a genuine friendship. I will always be thankful to her for everything.

Rhino moved in two weeks before the semester commenced. His first night there, we sat around our kitchen table while enjoying a bottle of Grey Goose.

"What do you like to do for fun, Rhino?" I said.

"Hmm. I bought a bike this summer and have been putting on twenty miles a day, three or four times a week."

My dad had just given me one of his bikes to ride because the one I was using had become inoperable.

"Well, that's pretty dope. Would you have any interest in going for a ride sometime?"

"Is the pope Catholic?" he replied. This was one of just a few witticisms I learned from Rhino. He was never one to shy away from a quote.

Rhino and I soon began going for rides around St. Cloud. We would ride through campus where everyone looked at us oddly because the majority of the time we had our shirts off. We maneuvered our way up the Beaver Island Trail, reaching as far as the I-94 highway. We soon moved out of the campus area toward Sauk Rapids, eventually encumbering a monster hill that took every ounce of effort to overcome.

Rhino and I formed a common bond in riding. I had never met someone who had enjoyed riding as much as he did. He inspired me to want to ride more and become more involved with the process. He was way ahead of where I was as a rider. The bike he purchased that summer was brand-new, fit with all the modern technological advances. The bike my dad had given me was a quality one, but an older model. Neither of us had three-thousand-dollar bicycles, but we didn't need that type of technology. We were satisfied with bikes that could ride. As long as we had that, we were set.

* * *

As school neared, we both decided that we should take things a step further. It was fun biking around the area, but both of us being athletes, we wanted to take on a new challenge. After some talk, Rhino proposed going to South Haven, specifically La La's, a fantastic burger joint. South Haven was fifteen miles outside of St. Cloud. It would not be an enormous distance to cover, but it also signaled that we were no longer biking recreationally. We had built up some stamina from our previous rides, so that Friday we went. As my good friend Mason says, "Set the date and do it. Don't wait around for the perfect day." We weren't waiting for anything on this day.

The ride to South Haven began much more difficult than expected. Riding down the Beaver Island Trail toward the highway was the easy part because trees covered us the whole time, blocking the wind from affecting our pace. As soon as we got off the trail and past the highway, reality hit us smack in the face. We made our way past St. Augusta and into farm country. The wind was constantly blowing in from the parallel fields. Adding to that, it was late August, and it was beastly hot. It took us two hours just to get the fifteen miles to South Haven.

We pulled into South Haven, locking our bikes on a stop sign adjacent to La La's. We went inside to eat. Not long after I was halfway through my first Grey Goose Redbull, my back seized up, forcing me to stand up and awkwardly stretch in front of the whole restaurant, all the while pondering if this ride was actually a good idea. I was in so much pain that I thought about quitting my day job and becoming a bum. Again, I worked at 4:00 a.m. unloading trucks at UPS, which was excruciating manual labor. Looking back, I should have stretched immediately after I got off my bike. If I did that, maybe I would not have serendipitously quit my job.

Through all my agony, I was still embracing our time in South Haven. It sucked feeling like I couldn't walk, much less bike home. Still, a little voice in my head kept saying, "*You love this, Q! You fucking love this!*" Yes, that voice was right. I sucked down a few more Grey Goose Redbulls, combined with three aspirins, and scampered back to my bike.

The subsequent ride home could not have gone any smoother, save for one event. My back loosened up, and we had the wind at our back. We made it back to St. Augusta sooner than expected and stopped at a small bar. The place was relatively empty, so we grabbed a table at the back. A waitress approached us and asked for our order.

"Can I get two Grey Goose Redbulls please?" I said.

"Of course," she replied. I went to grab some cash from the ATM. As I was waiting for my money to dispense, I looked over and saw her mixing the drinks with Ketel One vodka and a Monster energy drink. I was furious.

She marched back with our drinks and placed them on the table. "Um, excuse me. I don't mean to be rude, but these drinks aren't what I asked for," I said in a snippy tone.

Quickly she retorted, "Well, we don't carry either Grey Goose or Redbull." I told her it was fine and then rolled my eyes as soon as she turned around. I am the least picky person, except when it comes to alcohol. You can cook my steak too much or too little and I won't even notice. You can give me fries instead of onion rings and I won't flinch. Yet as soon as I am deprived of my sacred Grey Goose, mentally I become enraged and lose all patience.

The Grey Goose fetish was a bad habit of mine. While everyone else was buying Karkov or Taaka, I always went for the top shelf. I did this not only because Grey Goose was exceptional but also because it was a standard I set for myself. Someone once told me, "Live your life being the person you want to be, not the person you are." This is why I dabbled in expensive liquor and sexually liberated women. It was the life I wanted to live. I didn't have a lot of free cash to buy Grey Goose, but I budgeted for it. I didn't love having sex with random people, but it made me feel like the person I wanted to be. That was enough to appease my soul.

I sucked down my drink as fast as I could so we could leave. Rhino had a brief conversation with a pair of smokers outside. I unlocked our bicycles from the hand railing leading up to the bar, and we were gone in a matter of minutes. Disregarding the horrendous pit stop at the bar in St. Augusta, we cut our time in half on the way home. I was elated to the point that I felt like calling my dad to brag about what we accomplished. Again, my dad is the reason I even have a bike. He started me on training wheels at a very young age. By the time I was in middle school, he was taking me on trips from our home in Osseo to my Uncle Ben's place in Coon Rapids. These rides were no small feat, totaling roughly thirty miles. I owed most of what I knew about biking, which admittedly was very little, to my dad.

Rhino and I arrived back in St. Cloud just before sunset. I ran into an old friend of mine on campus, so we told him about where we had just been.

"Oh no! Q, you didn't! You're crazy, man!" he said.

Maybe we were crazy. Or maybe we were just getting started.

* * *

The next morning, I awoke feeling surprisingly good. I thought my legs might feel like mush, incapable of functioning that day. Instead, I was refreshed and feeling like I could do another ride. It was a Saturday, a day I typically reserved for hanging out with the neighbors and having a few cocktails.

This Saturday was different. Rhino awoke feeling in as good of spirits as I. We decided to get lunch at Benton Station, a nearby bar. We had a couple drinks, including a pleasant conversation with a rotund, older woman and a younger man.

"We were going to go to this place up the road for lunch, but the place wasn't even open. I just bought coupons on Groupon too," Rhino began.

"That place hasn't been open for a few months now. Bad management ran it into the ground," the woman noted.

The two said they had recently seen us riding around town on a number of occasions. It felt nice to be recognized. It validated the fact that our biking wasn't only interesting to us but to other people as well.

We finished our respective meals and cheerful conversation with the man and woman. It felt right to not go home and continue riding because the weather was superb.

"Let's go until we find another bar," suggested Rhino.

We decided to keep riding until we found that next bar. We took a trail through Sauk Rapids that eventually led us to railroad tracks and a feeling of being lost. We had no clue where we were. After finding some back roads, we thought we might never find another bar and only further distance ourselves from St. Cloud. We soon met a sign that indicated we were in Watab County. It was getting later in the afternoon, but we were determined to find a restaurant.

After another half hour, we were right next to Highway 10. We could have stopped and turned around, but the consensus was to keep going until we found a spot, no matter how long it took. Across the highway was a small neighborhood that we passed through. I could smell the coals burning, meaning some family was lucky enough to be cooking barbecue. After the neighborhood, we found a gas station. Rhino went in to inquire about nearby stopping points.

He came out after a few minutes. "The woman in there told me that Rice is only two miles ahead," he said.

To Rice we then traversed. The roads leading into Rice were under construction, so we had to cross back over Highway 10 again. Upon entering Rice, there were hundreds of people in the streets, including a live band. We stopped a police officer to ask what was going on.

"You're not from the area, are you, guys?" he said.

I looked at him confused. "No, sir. We biked here from the St. Cloud State campus."

The police officer returned my confused look before proceeding. "Well, it's Rice days right now, so that's why there are so many people here. Every bar should be pretty busy, so go and have a good time."

The sequence of events proved to be lucky for Rhino and I. If we had come to this small town any other weekend, we would not have run into all the hoopla that was happening.

Rice was an awesome city. The live music and people screaming at the top of their lungs reminded me of my hometown Osseo's annual town gathering. Every year they would put on the same ordeal and droves of people would come from all over to shop, drink, and listen to live bands.

The first bar we went into was jammed full of people. It was nearly impossible to wade through the masses, but eventually I made it to the counter and ordered two Grey Goose cranberries.

"Jesus Christ, this place is fucking packed, bro!" I shouted to Rhino.

"Yeah, and it's all old people," he replied.

"Well, dude, let's just finish this drink and go to a different spot."

After experiencing the succulence of the Grey Goose, we left and made our way across the street to O'Briens Pub, a wannabe Irish bar. The scene was similar to the one at the other bar in that it was full of older people and hard to find a spot. Fortunately, there were two open spots at the bar that Rhino and I managed to snag. A bartender with a busty chest approached us and asked what we wanted to drink.

"Two Grey Goose Redbulls," I replied.

"Ah, unfortunately we don't have Redbull. Is Monster okay?" Based off what happened the previous night, I politely declined the Monster energy drink and asked her to mix the Grey Goose with lemon sour instead.

The woman was very nice in her handling of us. She put our food order in right away, and we were eating within fifteen minutes. By now it was dark outside, and we still had to ride home. I leaned in close to her, partly to ask for directions home and partly to be closer to her breasts.

"You know, you have been so great to us all night. But I just have one more question. We aren't from around here and I'm wondering what would be the best way for us to bike home?"

She leaned in close, but her intentions weren't the same as mine. "It's actually really easy. All you have to do is cross over the train tracks over there," she said, pointing to the ones directly behind yet not visible to us. "Then you take a left and follow that road all the way and it will take you to St. Cloud."

I thanked her once again, left her a five-dollar bill, and then left the bar. All we had to do was cross the train tracks and then go left. If we did that, we would end up right back in St. Cloud. We returned to our bikes ready to leave when at that moment two women walked past us. The taller one with dark hair and I locked eyes in a lustful manner. "Hey there, stranger. I'm Georgia," was her introduction. With that, she had successfully made me mentally rework our plans to head home.

"Hey, hey. I'm Q, and this is my friend Rhino. How you guys doing tonight?"

The other woman, shorter and platinum blonde, then introduced herself as Nikki.

Georgia followed, "So what's with the bikes?"

I quickly thought to myself, *How can I make this sound cool?*

"Well, Georgia, Rhino and I biked here from campus. We stopped here and enjoyed the party a little bit and now we are going to have to ride back."

Two men passing by, one drunker than the other, jumped right into our conversation. He looked at me and then, pointing at Nikki, said, "Dude, is this your girlfriend?"

Instinctively, I put my arm around Georgia. "No, dude. But she is." The drunken man looked at me in distress, so I continued, "Yeah, so you guys have a good night, all right?" The man and his friend looked at each other, then sullenly left. I removed my arm from Georgia's shoulders and turned to face her.

Georgia looked at Nikki then at me. "Why don't you guys stay?"

I was replying to her question as soon as she said stay. "Oh, we will. Yeah, yeah. That sounds like a great time."

Georgia smiled, and then Nikki said, "We can go to my uncle's new bar just down the street."

The four of us made the half-mile walk to the outskirts of Rice. When we arrived at the bar, the bouncer greeted us with a disheveled look.

"IDs please," he muttered.

Nikki hesitantly announced, "I don't have my ID but the owner is my uncle. You can go and talk to him if you want." The bouncer glared at Nikki. He knew he should let her in to save his job, but he also had an ethical dilemma on his hands.

He left and, a few moments later, returned with Nikki's uncle in tow. "Nikki! How are you? Now I'm only letting you in this once, okay?" Nikki turned to Rhino and I, then back to her uncle.

"So I guess you're not twenty-one then, Nikki," I bellowed.

The whole situation made for an awkward conversation as I bought Georgia and I a drink, then found a table and sat down. "How old is Nikki?" I asked, turning to Georgia.

"She's twenty, but she will be twenty-one next month." I became reluctant to speak with Nikki after this because being with her felt like being her parent, having to watch over and monitor her behavior. The incident outside the bar affected the night, but the bar we were at was still a sight to behold.

It was like a scene straight out of the movie *Coyote Ugly*. Women were scantily clad and on top of the bars dancing to My Darkest Days' renowned song "Porn Star Dancing." These women would also pour shots into the mouths of willing men.

"They must be pouring the nastiest alcohol out of those bottles," I said to Rhino as he and Nikki had now joined us at the table.

This wild environment was beginning to become off-putting to Georgia and Nikki. Ten minutes had passed when Georgia turned to me. "We are going to go back to my house real quick and change."

"Are you coming back?" I anxiously replied.

"Yes. We definitely are, but Nikki wants to change because she has been wearing the same clothes all day."

Perplexed, I looked at Rhino and at my watch, and then said, "Well, it's almost eleven. Are you sure you are going to come back? If not, you can tell me, but I don't want to be waiting around here if you two aren't going to show up." Georgia assured me they would definitely be back, and the two hurriedly left.

Rhino began laughing, so I asked him what was so funny.

"Q, look at that guy over there at that table by himself." I looked at him but could find nothing noteworthy about him. Rhino continued, "I think one of those girls dancing up there is his girlfriend because he keeps looking at her and then stares at all the dudes that go up and get a drink from her."

I waited a few minutes, and then noticed that the man indeed was intently monitoring the dancer Rhino had pointed out. "Yeah, Rhino, I don't think that relationship is going to last too much longer."

"Well, no, but it's just funny how he is acting."

"I get it, Rhino. I'd be pissed off if I were him though."

Rhino looked at me curiously. "Well, why? She's just doing her job."

"I get that, but it doesn't mean that he should have to watch it. I mean look at her. She's practically naked and is surrounded by a bunch of horny men. Would you want to see that shit happen to your girl?"

I took a sip out of my drink and then checked my phone. Rhino was ranting about something, to which I tuned out. When I looked up from my phone, Georgia and Nikki had returned.

Georgia grabbed my hand and whispered into my ear, "Would you like to dance?"

We danced for the next couple of songs. My head began to spin as the combination of alcohol and rapid movement took effect.

Rhino and Nikki looked on, showing no signs of joining us. I went over to Rhino.

"Rhino, ask her to dance."

"I don't dance," he angrily replied. I couldn't force him to dance with her, but I knew that Nikki had wanted to dance.

I returned to Georgia when she asked, "Do you want to go outside?"

"You don't want to dance anymore?"

"I think I'm getting really hot, Q. Let's grab those two and leave."

Disappointed, I went over to our table and told them we were going to leave. At this point, I was fairly drunk and thought that I was going to get laid. Selfishly, I thought I deserved it after putting up with their inconsistent behavior. We went outside and Georgia said that she and Nikki should probably go home.

Sensing that I had to be assertive, "Can we come with? After all, it is a long way back to St. Cloud."

Georgia saw right through my master plan. "Actually you can't, Q."

After that, the vibe that was once so positive in our group began to disintegrate. Upset, I told Georgia we were leaving. She didn't stop me. The night was over and the connection I thought I had made disappeared, all because I didn't get to have sex with her. It was a testament to how selfish I was. I wasn't even willing to try to be friends with Georgia. As soon as I didn't get what I wanted, I had already moved on.

Before I moved to St. Cloud and adopted a more conceited personality, I would have tried to befriend Georgia and get to know her on a platonic level. Now it was all about me and what I wanted. As evidenced by this night, it didn't get me very far.

Rhino and I solemnly returned to our bikes in the same way the two drunken men from earlier sauntered away when I denied their chance at talking to Georgia and Nikki. The night didn't end as we both had hoped, but we still had to ride home.

I unfastened the by now annoying lock that juxtaposed our bikes. We took off into the night, away from Rice and all that night's events. Like most encounters I had that fall, I tried to put this one as far in the past as possible. Riding away from Rice made it easy to physically get away, but mentally, the night's events were right there with me.

We crossed over the railroad tracks and turned left onto the road that would bring us all the way back into St. Cloud. The night needed a spark. We couldn't let what had transpired earlier derail our fun.

"Q, get behind me! I'm the only one here with a bike light for Christ's sake," Rhino said.

"What's your point, Rhino?"

"My point? Ah, yeah, my point is that if we get pulled over, we will both get DUIs."

I chuckled. "Doubt it! The police aren't out here looking for bicyclists, bro!"

More time elapsed as we put Rice behind us. The lights of the few cars that passed were a boon to our sights. Rhino's bike light did the job, but predictably it didn't provide the visibility a car's headlights would. A police car passed us as we became parallel with the Mississippi River, and to Rhino's surprise, it did not stop.

"See, I told you, dude," I quietly murmured just loud enough for him to hear.

I doubt many people have rode past the Mississippi in the dead of night. It is a memorable sight seeing the moon's light glisten off the water. I was beginning to sober up. We stopped at an overlook of the river. The water didn't appear to move, even though rivers are constantly flowing. It seemed stuck in time, like myself. I turned to Rhino, who was urinating in a set of small bushes. I didn't say anything because he wasn't in this moment with me. For the next few minutes I stood awestruck, unable to believe the sensation that was coursing through my veins.

After a time, I too needed to urinate, but we soon reverted back to riding. With Rhino leading the way, we passed houses stationed along the river. A few dogs barked, but none made their presence more noticeable. We eventually passed over the same railroad. Here we knew where we were based on riding through earlier in the night.

It was then that momentum shifted in our favor. We furiously began pedaling, matching each other stride for stride. The night was becoming more beautiful as it became less noticeable. I was no longer taking the time to examine the scenery, yet it was still resonating with me. We were now in Sauk Rapids and only a few short miles from home. We went down the spiraling cement staircase that would bring us closer to the river. We then passed various homes and apartment complexes, arriving back in St. Cloud near downtown.

We passed the bars as 2:00 a.m. neared. There weren't many people out because school had not started yet. And then we were home. Our roommate Pinky was awake and curious why I was smiling and breathless.

"I'll tell you in the morning, Pinky."

I said good night to Rhino and climbed into bed, still unable to comprehend the beauty of what had just happened.

* * *

That ride still gives me chills. That was living in the moment, letting all care go and just riding my bicycle. There is something special about riding late at night. Not only are there few cars but also there are nearly no people. The loudest noises are the crickets chirping and the wheels of my bike, which violently churn at every stroke of the pedal. During the daylight, I am robbed of this blissful audibility.

After the social and physical experience we had going to and from Rice, we began to think bigger. Rhino approached me a few days later. "We should go to Brainerd. I was looking at Google Maps and it is only sixty miles away."

"What compelled you to look into that, Rhino?"

"I was just thinking about the other night and that if we rode the way we did back for a longer time, we could really put on some distance."

He was right. If we took this seriously enough, we could start to travel longer distances.

"I'm all for it. Let's go on Friday."

When Friday arrived, my angst was high. I knew we could do a trip of this magnitude, but sixty miles was no small feat. Rhino had things going on, so we didn't convene until two o'clock. We didn't *leave* until three in the afternoon.

Google Maps said it would take five hours to bike there, so before leaving, we figured we would make it to Brainerd around 8:00 p.m. Our ride there didn't start as anticipated. We were in Sauk Rapids when we hit construction. The workers were gone for the day, meaning it wasn't an active site, but going into the construction zone could have been dangerous.

"There is no other way, Rhino. We have to go through it. We can't backtrack right now," I said.

Mounds of dirt littered the middle of the site, but the outside was relatively clean.

"I think you're right. Let's just go straight through," Rhino agreed.

We were almost out of the construction zone when a loud bang emanated from my left. A worker had gotten out of his machine and looked in our direction. He said nothing, but I could sense he wasn't privy to what we were doing. We exited the construction zone safely but had lost considerable time with the delay.

Still, we were plugging away. The miles continued to tick off. We stopped to take a water break. I looked in my backpack and saw that I had forgotten a phone charger. Both of our phones had enough battery to get us to Brainerd, but not having them charged for the next day meant we would be riding blind for some time when our phones died.

I had packed a few water bottles, anticipating that we would encounter gas stations along the way.

Rhino stated, "We are thirty-five miles in. I don't know when we are going to see another store. I'm almost out of water."

Without hesitation, I gave him one of mine. I still had an extra one and half of my current one. I assumed we would find a place to stop before then.

A yard the size of approximately three football fields was soon on our right. A dog bolted from one end of the property to the next, although never coming near us. It looked like a guard dog, intent on ripping out our throats if we threatened to enter the property.

Unnerved, I noticed I was now down to my last water bottle, having now finished the other one. Things were beginning to look dire. We didn't know if we would find somewhere to get more water.

"I could eat the ass end of a boar pig," Rhino exclaimed.

We turned left and entered the city limits of Freedham. Shortly after, a sign appeared noting that a convenience store was just ahead on the left.

"Thank God!" Rhino exclaimed.

We turned left and saw the convenience store. Rhino slammed on his brakes and went toward the door.

"*Fuck!*" he shouted.

"What's up, dude?"

"It's closed." Outside the store was a machine with a large Pepsi can emblazoned on the front.

"Rhino, I bet there is water in there."

He walked over to the soda machine. "You've gotta be kidding me. It's only soda in here." There was only soda, but this was also our only viable drinking option.

"I don't know about you, but I'm going to drink a few sodas anyway. I don't know if we will have another stop before Brainerd," I said.

I reached into my pocket and grabbed a five-dollar bill. I bought two Mountain Dews and chugged them, unabashed. I gave Rhino the change and began to think about the rest of the ride. The sun was slowly setting, which meant it wasn't long before we would once again be riding in the darkness.

"Look at your phone. How many miles do we have left?" I urged Rhino.

"I would guess we have a little over twenty based off this map. I don't want to use my phone because you forgot a charger."

"Oh, Jesus Christ. Seriously? I just want to know if we are going in the right direction."

Rhino pointed at the pages from MapQuest he was holding. "I guarantee we are going in the right direction."

I trusted him. We had only been riding for a few hours, but I needed assurance we were going to get to Brainerd at a decent hour.

Soon after, a sign popped up saying Brainerd was twenty miles away. We knew now that we could stay on this road all the way to Brainerd. A few miles later, a massive bird became visible.

"Dude! It's an ostrich! What in the world is it doing up here?" I exclaimed.

Rhino disregarded the ostrich, saying, "I've seen plenty of those. People raise them in the country. It's nothing new."

I didn't think I would ever see another one, not since the time my parents took me to the zoo as a young boy. The last stretch to Brainerd became grueling. Hill upon hill forced us to find another layer of resiliency. The sun was almost set.

Looking behind me at Rhino, I said, "Well, one thing we have learned is that what goes up must come down."

Whenever we went up a hill, it was challenging, but when we would go down, we barely had to pedal. I was in mid laughter when a dog sprang out from a yard on my left. I hurried past before it could make an attempt at my life. I was turning my left shoulder to look back for Rhino when he whizzed past me, shouting "Holy shit!" The dog was not going to catch us, but the fact it tried was enough to scare Rhino into pedaling his ass off.

"I could eat the ass end of a boar pig," Rhino once again uttered when I caught up with him.

"Do you say anything else, bro? God. I could have eaten when we were in Freedham. These granola bars aren't doing shit for me."

The sun was now set and we still weren't to Brainerd. A pair of tall posts with red lights blinking came into view. After that, street-lights began to appear. In the next ten minutes, we were on the outskirts of Brainerd, ironically passing a building with the Pepsi logo displayed on it.

We took a right at the next stoplight and began downhill toward the business sector of Brainerd. We passed a massive, albeit closed, convention center. What followed was a Snap Fitness on the right and a Holiday gas station on the left. We wanted to stop at the first bar we could find. This time it was TJ's Log Cabin.

"Can I see your IDs please?" asked the hefty bartender. She took our drink orders. An older couple was sitting on our right and the man glared at me when I sat down. "So what are you guys up to tonight?" asked the bartender when she returned with our drinks.

"We just biked here from St. Cloud," I answered.

The old man then nodded, although neither approvingly or disapprovingly. It was more a nod that said, "Okay, you're decent enough people."

Halfway through my first Grey Goose Redbull, I whipped out my phone. "Rhino, smile for the camera!" After choosing which photo out of the four I liked best, I posted it to Facebook.

"I'm kind of curious to see what people think of this," I said, chugging my first drink like it was going to be my last.

On my left, a young man with glasses was staring intently at me. Two heavy women surrounded him. I initially looked back to come off as cordial. He wouldn't stop looking at me, which made me uncomfortable.

"Dude, this guy keeps looking at me, Rhino."

Rhino looked over at him. "He's not looking at you."

"Dude, yes he is."

Rhino looked over again, took another drink, and said, "He's probably gay."

Rhino's statement made sense to me. Why else would this guy be staring so intently at me? I didn't mind the fact that he was looking at me, but did he have to be so obvious? It then occurred to me that I probably did the same thing to some poor woman at one point. I brushed off my bother with the man. We paid our tabs and left.

"Q, I can get us a room at the Rodeway Inn for eighty dollars. That's forty dollars apiece."

Unlocking our bikes, I said, "I'm cool with that. Thank God for Expedia."

The Rodeway Inn was on the other side of Brainerd. We eased back into riding, careful not to overexert our relaxed muscles. We were able to take sidewalks most of the way, but after passing a Walgreens, we were forced onto the shoulder of a busy road. After getting sidetracked and ending up at a Polaris dealership, we finally arrived at the Rodeway Inn.

"Wait outside while I go in," Rhino said. "The room is only booked for one person, so I don't want to get charged extra if you come in with me."

After Rhino was in, I peeked through the door and saw him talking to an older Middle Eastern man. Rhino returned shortly after, and we snuck around the back to enter the hotel. This would become common for us on trips because the great deals he scored on Expedia were only possible because he was booking the rooms for one individual.

We rolled our bikes into the room. I jumped on the bed and was ready to relax.

"Hey, let's go to the liquor store," an annoying voice blurted out.

"Rhino, it's past ten. The stores are closed now."

"No, let's just try."

I sat up and tried to reason. "Rhino, I know in cheese country things are different, but here liquor stores close at ten. Just trust me."

Rhino paced back and forth. "Well, then let's go to a grocery store."

Unwilling to argue, I agreed to walk to a nearby Cub Foods in search of liquor.

The walk there was sketchy. We passed a younger man who was just finishing his shift at Kohls, as evidenced by the jangling of his keys and the putrid smell of his black t-shirt. To get to Cub Foods, we had to cross Highway 371. Running through the wet, dirty grass that led to the highway, I thought how much more enjoyable being in the hotel would have been. Rhino tried to walk into the liquor store but was denied by the sliding door that wouldn't slide.

At Cub Foods, I bought a box of five-dollar granola bars, even though their satiation factor was low. I found Rhino perusing the beer aisle, which was sad considering this wasn't ordinary beer. It was 3.2 beer, meaning it was practically not worth drinking. Rhino opted for a six-pack of Mike's Hard Lemonade.

Back outside, I saw a Mexican restaurant worth checking out.

"No, I have to get back and drink this before it gets warm," Rhino growled.

I laughed thinking about how idiotic that sounded. We returned to the hotel and I cozied up in bed. Before I knew it, I was asleep, thinking about the possibilities of the next day.

* * *

The next morning I awoke to the sound of Stan Verrett on SportsCenter. Rhino had forgotten to shut off the TV because when I turned to look at him, the remote was sitting right next to his face, fortunately far enough to avoid the drool that was seeping out of his mouth. The clock read 9:12 a.m.

"Rhino, wake up."

Rhino took his time getting out of bed like always. His routine consisted of sleeping for ten more minutes, then rolling over to check his phone.

"We got to get going, dude. Check out is at eleven," I mentioned.

We prepared to leave the hotel. SportsCenter had turned into actual sports as the World Cup of basketball aired in the background.

"You aren't going to brush your teeth?" Rhino asked.

"Well, considering I didn't bring a phone charger, do you honestly think a toothbrush was high on my list?"

I never brushed my teeth on these trips, mostly because I always forgot to pack the necessary materials. I figured the alcohol would mitigate my putrid breath.

We returned outside to the cool fall breeze. It was still morning, so the sun hadn't fully staked its claim on the day. Having just gone through a long ride not even twenty-four hours earlier, Rhino and I were more equipped to handle the day. We went to a Super America gas station and loaded up on enough bottled water to last us until St. Cloud. I bought a small box of Nutri Grain bars.

"Do you want to get some lunch?" I asked Rhino.

"Sure. What do you have in mind?"

"Well, there was an Erbs and Gerbs just back there," I said, pointing in the direction of our hotel. "We will have to backtrack a little, but a sandwich sounds good."

We locked our bikes onto a handicapped parking sign at the nearby Wells Fargo. The store wasn't busy at all. I ordered first.

"Um, hi. Can I have a Girf and a cup for water?"

"Actually, sir," the beefy cashier began, "we are out of water right now because the whole town is on a water watch."

"What does that mean?" I questioned.

"Essentially, we had some bad water get into the system, so the city is limiting everyone's water use."

I instantly thought of the shower I took that morning and how my body was now probably lined with mold and dirty water.

I was only able to procure a sandwich, but it was enough. We left Brainerd the same way we came. It was Saturday morning and the traffic was insane compared to the night before. We tried our best to stay on sidewalks and out of the road, but at times that was impossible.

We crossed over near the same convention center and headed for the back roads. We were only a few miles out of Brainerd when all the fluids I consumed to replace what I deprived my body of the previous night suddenly needed to be excreted.

"Dude, we have to pull over!" I said to Rhino.

"What? Already?"

"Bro, if I don't, I might piss my pants."

We pulled off to the side of the road. No one was around now, ironic considering there was just plenty of traffic. I was midstream when a car pulled onto the shoulder on the opposite side of the road. *What the fuck is this idiot doing?* I thought to myself. This idiot was driving a black Volkswagen. I couldn't see his face, but he was by himself and had picked the worst place to pull over.

"Rhino, what is this guy's deal?" I turned to see a line of urine coming from his midsection. "Sorry. Never mind, dude."

I finished doing my thing. Rhino soon followed. As soon as we continued on, the car drove off.

"Doesn't that guy know that timing is everything?" I joked.

We continued without many annoyances. It was decided that we were going to try a faster route home. This meant attempting to circumvent all the minimal maintenance roads we encountered the previous day. Our plan was working. It wasn't deathly hot yet, we were on paved roads, and we were near the halfway point.

Soon a large turn approached. I didn't know it at the time, but on this massive turn, we were supposed to turn left at some point. Rhino was behind me yelling. I couldn't make out his words. His voice was getting louder as I sensed he was closer.

"*Turn here!*" were his words I finally caught.

I looked up from my stride and noticed a pickup truck coming into view in the other lane. I panicked, fearing I might miss my turn or cut off the truck. Instead of doing the logical step, which would have been to stop and wait for the truck to pass, I kept pedaling. Seeing that there was no safe way to turn, I became wobbly, losing control of my bike. I slid off the pavement and onto the dirt shoulder. The dirt and gravel took hold of my tires and would not relinquish. A few seconds after that, I was in the ditch and heading straight toward a small pond.

Luckily, my brakes began to work again just before I went into the water. Screeching to a halt, I turned around and saw Rhino on the road, pointing and laughing.

Rejoining him back where I should have been, he asked, "Q, what the hell was that?"

Embarrassed, I didn't even try to answer. Rhino hazed me for a few more moments as we got back to riding.

We continued on for the rest of the ride home without any issues until Rhino's phone died and we were without direction. We turned off the road that would have brought us back to the construction zone too early. We were now in Sartell, but only a handful of miles from home. I looked at Rhino and noticed his face was peeling.

"Dude, your face looks like a tomato."

"I know. Don't remind me. I didn't buy sunscreen."

"Well, do you usually burn so easily?"

"Yes."

"I guess I don't understand why you didn't pack sunscreen," I said, confused.

"Because I forgot. Come look at my lips. Are they peeling?"

I looked at Rhino's lips and indeed they were peeling. It looked like dried toothpaste that he was too lazy to wipe off.

Hesitantly and resisting laughter, I said, "They're peeling a little, but it isn't anything to worry about I think."

It was midafternoon now, so we made a stop for dinner at a place called Molitor's. I spent another thirty dollars I didn't have on alcohol and low-grade bar food. Still, the realization that we were going to have biked 120 miles in two days suddenly dawned on me. It was a soothing feeling, one that carried me happily all the way home.

CHAPTER THREE

The trip to Brainerd was awesome, but there was no way it was going to be our biggest accomplishment. Like anything, the more you practice, the better you subsequently become. Rhino and I were rearing for another quest. Throughout the next week, we had discussions about where we could go.

"Do we head toward the cities?" I asked.

"That might be too busy. Let's just look in a different direction than Brainerd," suggested Rhino.

Simple overhead views of Google Maps led to us eventually settling on North Branch. North Branch was a little further, around the seventy-mile range. It'd be the same type of ride as Brainerd, only we would be more prepared. We planned to leave at a decent hour and bring more than enough water. Plus, the aforementioned and mechanically inclined Mason was coming along, meaning we had a true outdoorsman accompanying us.

That Friday morning came, exactly one week after the Brainerd trip. Anticipation was running rampant among us. Yet somehow, through our own doing and Thirsty Thursday's entrapment, we didn't get going until 2:00 p.m. This was a frustrating reality. I thought we had learned from the previous week, but our immaturity evidently took precedence over our goals. Fortunately, we did survey our route and knew there was no way we were going to cross any gravel roads. It was also a relatively straight shot from St. Cloud to North Branch, and hills were supposed to be minimal. We were set to go four miles up Highway 23 out of St. Cloud toward Duluth before hanging a right onto highway 95. From there it would literally be the straight shot we were anticipating.

It was still early in the school year, and I hadn't properly caught up with Mason. We were a ways out of St. Cloud, the late afternoon sun beating down on us, when I asked him, "So, dude! Tell me about your summer. Any ladies I should know about?"

"Q, even if there were any ladies, I wouldn't tell you because I know you would tell *everybody*."

"Woah, Mase Daddy, I think you have me mistaken for some- one else."

A small smirk shone across Mason's face. "No. I think I have it right, Q. If I tell you what I did with my summer, I might as well just say *see ya* to any chance of that staying between us."

At this point Rhino interjected. "Mason, why won't you just tell us? Why? Seems a little weird to me."

Rhino said this in a nonjesting manner, which was typical. He had a way with words, but most of the time it got him into trouble. This time Mason was the bear you never wanted to poke, and Rhino poked away.

"Oh, God. Ryan, just stay out of this," Mason snapped.

"I don't get it. I just don't get it. As my dad used to say, 'Weird, but true,'" Rhino said in a hazing manner.

I tried to sway the conversation toward the subject of me, think- ing it would lighten the mood.

"Well, Mason, I happened to have a little fling this summer. It didn't last that long, but, eh, it was something to do."

"Well, that's good, Q. I'm happy for you," Mason replied in a fatherly voice.

Mason was always the father figure in our friend group even if his actions suggested otherwise. Standing nearly six feet tall, he had a belly, yet an even bigger beard, and heart. This was part of what made this trip so interesting. We could banter back and forth among the three of us, and then laugh it off as soon as the conversation became too nasty or insulting toward one person in particular.

We pulled into Princeton around dinnertime ready for a meal. None of us had ever been to Princeton before, so we had no idea of the quality dinner spots. We stopped outside of the American Legion. Three older men were smoking cigarettes. They all wore raggedy flannels. Their presence made me swivel my head to see what else was within sight.

I saw a large building that appeared to be a restaurant right next to the roundabout we had just exited. We rode over, locked our bikes, and headed in. The place was busy, but we were able to find three spots open at the bar.

"How are we doing tonight?" a young woman asked as she approached us. "You guys look like you just came from some type of event."

"We are biking to North Branch," Mason quipped as he took off his backpack that carried two liters of water.

"Well, that's impressive. What made you guys stop here?"

"Grey Goose and hopefully food," I intruded.

The bartender was making our drinks when Mason inexplicably stood from his chair and began doing full stretching exercises at the bar. The other people in the restaurant looked at him like he had a small bird in his beard.

"What the hell is he doing?" Rhino asked me, half laughing, half embarrassed.

"I have no idea," I said as I tried to bury my face in my newly arrived Grey Goose.

"Mason, stop doing that," I said to him, trying not to let the other people watching know I was embarrassed.

Mason's stretching routine consisted of him spreading his legs as far apart as possible and rocking side to side. Needless to say, he wasn't going to be confused with one of those guys you'd see on an in-home fitness DVD.

Mason eventually returned to his seat. We ate our dinner somewhat quietly. The bartender gave us each a complimentary drink, which was completely unnecessary but indicated that she liked some combination of our presence.

"Where are you guys biking to?" a customer yelled at us from across the bar.

"To North Branch, sir," Mason replied.

"Well, you guys better get going. The sun is going to set soon."

"Sir, we aren't afraid of a little night riding."

"Well, young man, out here you never know what can happen."

We paid our tabs and exited the building. After unlocking our bikes and noticing the fast descending sunset, we headed further into the downtown portion of Princeton.

"Are you sure you guys don't want a hat or gloves?" I asked Rhino and Mason. "It sure is going to get chilly tonight."

"I maybe could go for some gloves, but otherwise I'll be all right," Rhino retorted confidently.

"All right. Your guys' loss."

We continued for two miles outside of the city when all of a sudden we hit a dead end. I was in charge of directions, so I quickly pulled out my printed turn-by-turn instructions.

"What the fuck, Q? Where are we?" the two of them frustratingly asked.

I didn't know. I frantically looked for a mistake on my part.

"I don't know what's going on," I said softly.

After looking at the map more, I realized we had started in the wrong direction. It was a straight shot to North Branch, yet somehow I forgot that fact. I had us going in the completely wrong direction.

"Fellas, we are going to have to turn around. We were supposed to stay straight through that roundabout instead of turning off. My bad."

The two met my statement with expected disdain. Still, we had to turn around and head back. We stopped at a Casey's gas station, where both Rhino and Mason nonchalantly bought a pair of gloves.

When we finally got going in the right direction, the sun was on its way down. It didn't matter, at least to me.

"Come on. We are close enough to North Branch, guys," I said encouragingly.

We all knew we were going to make it. Collectively, we put our heads down and rode hard. We passed through a construction zone.

A stop sign was lit up in red to inform drivers of their whereabouts. For us, it was a quick turn of the head to the right and then to the left, followed by speeding through the intersection. Mason led the way as we made no stops until we arrived in a small city ten miles away from North Branch for a drink. It was now pitch black outside.

"Q, you go in while Mason and I smoke," said Rhino while gesturing toward the bar.

I went into the small bar that was packed with older people. It was uneventful and all the old timers were now staring at me. An old woman approached me.

"What can I get you?"

Intimidated, I simply ordered a bottle of beer. Rhino and Mason soon traipsed in. Our stay was uneventful. They each ordered a beer and then left because the crowd was not to our standards. Outside, Rhino booked us a hotel on Priceline.

"That means you each owe thirty dollars."

"Don't worry," I replied. "You will get your money."

We had a place to stay for the night, so all we had to do was get there. Ten miles was all that stood between North Branch and us. These ten miles would further enhance my love for bicycling. What in reality took over an hour, the ten miles felt like only a couple of minutes. Rhino and Mason's bike lights led the way. They were strong enough to make oncoming traffic turn off their powerful overhead lights. Our bikes synchronized with the night, allowing us to smoothly travel our path and not upset the calmness that the night sky had already provided. We put our trust in society, convinced that no drunk drivers would blindside us on a long, winding turn.

I looked up into the sky at the magnificent sight, embracing the small planets for their sheer beauty. Nothing could trump the moment I was in. I have never been one for science, but even I could appreciate the foregrounding astronomy.

Before I knew it, the ecstasy of the moment was over and we were pulling into North Branch. At this point, my lower back was sorer than Rhino after he loses in Madden.

"I think it's because you're so freaking tall," the sagacious Mason suggested.

As we stopped at the first bar located in downtown North Branch, I couldn't help but mutter to myself how lucky I was to have Mason as a friend. Like anyone, he had his quirks, but he was a genuine soul who always had my back.

We didn't stay long at the bar because of the predictable lack of excitement. We then left and went to our hotel. Rhino and Mason checked in while I stayed outside. We took care of business and soon I was falling asleep to the sound of the TV. We had done it again.

* * *

Waking up the next morning, I felt better. My back pain had vanished. I was ready to go home. We checked out of the hotel. The weather was glorious; not too hot but definitely a lot of sun. Our day seemed primed for greatness until we began riding out of the parking lot.

"Oh no," Mason groaned.

I looked over and his back tire was flat. His bike could barely move forward. There was no way he was going to be able to ride on that faulty tire. We pulled into the Taco Bell parking lot to escape embarrassment from onlookers.

"We need to find a bike shop," I proclaimed.

"Do you honestly think this place is going to have one?" Mason uttered rather dejectedly.

Rhino whipped out his phone. Moments later, he deadpanned the truth we all expected but didn't want to hear: "They don't have one."

"What do you think we should do?" I asked to no one in particular.

Mason's gaze went across the street. "Let's go over there."

Mason led us to a hardware store. Inside they had plenty of tools, but not many that could help us out. Mason's bike model was older, and this store didn't have the tools we needed. After some conversation with a younger man who was working the cash register, he agreed to let us work on fixing the flat tire in the back, provided we paid for the materials.

35

For over an hour, Mason grappled with his bicycle while Rhino and I stood helplessly to the side. Mason was the only one who had any idea how to fix a popped inner tube. He struggled to keep air inflated in his tire. It was now past noon, and we had to begin thinking of alternative plans.

"What a joke," Mason complained as we walked out. "That place literally had nothing. Anywhere else and I guarantee I could have fixed my tube."

We went over to an O'Reilly Auto Parts, and they too were unable to help. I began calling friends back in St. Cloud, but none of them could be a remedy to our situation.

We ate lunch at a Mexican restaurant. I spent the duration of the meal continuing to try to procure a ride for us. It was simply a lot to ask of someone. The pitch, "Hey, friend! Can you come pick us up in North Branch? I'll pay for your gas and buy you a case of beer. Oh, and also your car has to fit three bikes in it." This phrasing soon got very old.

We left the restaurant to go across the highway to a Nike outlet store. We weren't in there for two minutes before a scrawny teenager approached.

"Hey, fellas! Are you looking at shoes today? Can I grab a size for anyone?" Not being in the mood, I rudely ignored him and walked away.

I waited outside the store with Mason while Rhino continued to look around the store.

"Mason, I think I'm going to have to call Sammy."

Mason's face became serious.

"No. Don't call Sammy. I can't handle him."

Sammy was a guy I met the previous year at a house party. There was nothing wrong with Sammy, except that he was extremely clingy and creepy. One time at a party, he was watching Scooter make out with a girl he really liked.

After seeing what happened, he went up to Scooter, awestruck, and asked, "Dude, how did you do that?"

Since then, he has idolized Scooter and, for some reason, me as well.

What Sammy did have, besides an irritating personality, was a truck. I knew his truck would fit all our bikes and allow us to get home.

"Mason, he might be our last option."

Mason looked away. He knew what had to be done.

I dialed up Sammy and the line began ringing.

"Hello?" answered Sammy in a confused tone.

"Sammy, what are you up to, my man?"

"Watching college football and having some beers. Why?" he asked in an excited tone.

"Well, Sammy, I'm in a bind and I could sure use your help. You see, two friends and I biked out to North Branch and one of them has a flat tire. We could really use a ride. I was wondering if you could help. I'll pay for your gas and buy you a case of beer."

Some time elapsed before Sammy answered. "Q, I'll do it. Give me some time and I will be there in over an hour."

I hung up the phone and told Rhino and Mason the news. "All I know is I'm not sitting in the front seat," said Mason.

"Guys, be nice. I know Sammy is not your favorite, but he is really helping us out."

For the next hour and a half, the three of us sat on a curb out-side of Target. We laughed as we ripped on each other for various personality defects. It quickly became the high point of our day.

"Mason, you know the reason your tire popped, right?" Rhino asked. Mason punching him on the arm was cause enough to realize the answer would not portray Mason in a nice light.

A feeling of worthlessness consumed me. "You know what, fel-las? I honestly feel like we are homeless, just sitting on the side of the road right now. People are probably looking at us and laughing."

I knew we weren't that grungy looking, but it wasn't far off to think that thought crossed some people's minds.

Soon Sammy arrived in his silver pickup. We exchanged pleas-antries and loaded our bikes into the back. I filled Sammy's gas tank and we were ready to head back to St. Cloud.

"How did you guys get out here? Did you know I'm from here?" were the first things Sammy said once we got on the highway.

"I didn't, dude. That's pretty cool" was all I could say.

Mason and Rhino were whispering to each other, which bothered me because they were purposefully trying to make me do all the talking.

"Man, these mile markers sure go by fast when you are in a car," I remarked to Sammy.

By now Mason and Rhino were asleep, although Mason later admitted he was pretending to avoid entering the awkward conversation Sammy and I had. Then Sammy directed the conversation in an expected but unpleasant direction.

"So you know Sasha, right?" said Sammy with genuine inquisitiveness.

I knew what he wanted to talk about. Sammy had slept with Sasha, and he wanted to leave no doubt that I was aware of this fact. I did like Sasha, but I didn't like where this conversation was heading.

"I do know her. We know her friends Mariah and Alyssa. They used to party at our place last year and then this summer."

"Well, did you know I took her virginity?" deadpanned Sammy.

"Um, no, I did not," I said, looking in the backseat to see if either of my friends had awoken.

"Well, yeah, I did that. It was awesome," continued Sammy.

"That's great for you, man. Just great." Silence ensued. "I actually hooked up with Alyssa," I said, regretting it as soon as I said it.

A look of jealousy crept onto Sammy's face, similar to the one I saw when Scooter and Sammy's crush were sharing lips.

"Oh, really?" was all Sammy could muster. "How was that?" he asked slowly.

"Well, we don't need to go in depth about it, Sammy."

I did not want to share intimate details with Sammy. Knowing him, if I told him anything, he would run straight to whomever he wanted and start blabbing.

We were now close to St. Cloud when Sammy instigated more unnecessary banter.

"Do you want to talk more about Sasha?"

Sasha, again, was a great woman. I could not say a bad word about her. The thing about it was Sasha was a tad overweight. Also, the last time I saw Sasha, she was belligerently drunk and stuck in the sink of our house. Naturally, I found this hilarious. At present, Sammy attempting to brag about his escapade with Sasha could in no way be construed as impressive. Again, nothing against anyone, but Sammy was definitely overreaching on this one.

I slyly deflected more questions about Sasha, trying to preserve everyone's integrity. We had made it back to St. Cloud. We dropped off our bikes at Mason's place and then I took Sammy to the liquor store to buy him some beer. A long, exhausting day that entailed virtually no bike riding was mercifully coming to an end. Yet all things considered, it was a memorable weekend.

CHAPTER FOUR

The misfortune in North Branch took a lot out of us emotionally. In the ensuing weeks, Mason, in his drunken stupor, had managed to crash his bike and wreck his rim, rendering him incapable of riding with us for the rest of the season. Rhino and I continued to ride around the St. Cloud area, but as far as major trips, we hadn't planned anything. Everyone had other things to do, so it was unreasonable to expect to be able to take a long ride every weekend. It wasn't until late October that we eventually got back out there again.

Before we began, Rhino and I deemed it to be our last ride of the season. We were headed for Alexandria (or Alex, as the locals referred to it), a trip that was estimated to be in the seventy-mile range again. It was the perfect ride because the Lake Wobegon Trail would take us the whole way there once we got out of St. Cloud and into St. Joseph.

This time, Rhino and I did it right. We left early in the morning and had the necessary supplies. Since it was late October, I knew we were dealing with one of the last nice days of the season. The sun beat down upon us all day but not in an uncomfortable way. It was nice enough to wear only a light sweatshirt and shorts. Rhino's body, being blessed with profuse perspiration, broke out before lunch.

We rode that day with a purpose. The trail was magnificent. We passed lakes, farmland, and various small cities. Seemingly nothing was going to slow us down.

"What do you think about Ebola?" Rhino asked.

"Why do you ask? That's kind of random."

"I mean, do you have Ebola?"

I was thinking Rhino was just trying to pass the time. "Well, obviously it is a horrible disease. Recently, I hear they have been able to treat people though."

"Well, yeah, but do you have Ebola?" Rhino asked once again.

I wasn't even going to begin to satirize his bravado. Ebola struck national headlines in the fall of 2014, which was weird because a simple Google search revealed that the disease first originated in 2009. The only reason it was making headlines at the time was because a few Americans had contracted the disease. The whole perceived epidemic proved how fickle the western media is. As soon as the virus was believed to be outside of the United States, the media paid no more attention to it, even though the disease was still ravaging African nations. Needless to say, Rhino's attempt to put light on the situation was not entertaining.

"You know, Rhino, people are dying from this disease."

"Well, yeah, but who cares?" he wondered aloud.

Disease has always been a tough subject for me to approach. I have always considered myself lucky to not have a terminal illness or lifelong affliction, especially with all the sexual partners I had in the last year. There were many mornings I would wake up after a hook up and wonder if I had just contracted chlamydia. Even though I harped on myself to be responsible and not so whimsical with my escapades, I still wouldn't think twice about hooking up with a random woman. The craving for exotic, serendipitous experiences overpowered my common sense.

I'd have nightmares about waking up and my life not being the same, having either contracted a sexually transmitted infection or being responsible for an unplanned pregnancy. It was an indictment of how out of control of my sexuality I had become. The fear of risking my future couldn't save me from my impulses and immaturity.

I have always felt sorry for those that do have an affliction of any type. Modern medicine is great, but it unfortunately cannot solve all that ails the world. I wasn't going to try to make Rhino share my sentiments. I could only hope that one day his ignorance would change.

About halfway to Alexandria, we stopped for a long lunch in Sauk Centre to meet Scooter, who was in the city delivering packages for FedEx. It was there that I made a critical mistake. While sipping on a Grey Goose Redbull, I took a few too many ibuprofens to keep my back loose. The combination of the alcohol and the pills made me behave strangely. I began laughing uncontrollably. Rhino and Scooter looked at each other, confused, as I began mocking many things they said.

"Q, are you okay?" Scooter finally asked.

"I think I'm all right. I mean, I only had two drinks and like six ibuprofen."

Rhino and Scooter looked at each other and then chuckled. We stayed at the restaurant for a good hour while I waited for my mind-altering buzz to subside. Once again my own stupidity hurt us on our time.

We eventually said good-bye to Scooter and hopped back on the trail. The beautiful fall weather was in full swing, and I was grateful that I was able to refocus and still enjoy the cool breeze and Halloween flair that had engulfed Sauk Centre and its neighboring cities.

It reminded me that traveling was a big deal. It benefits an individual to see different things because it makes you more cultured and cognizant of things outside the normal realm of your everyday life. Biking afforded me that opportunity. Working on a college budget, it would have been tough to take trips to see the Eiffel Tower or go to Cancun during spring break.

This was another reason why biking was so special. Biking is free. I don't pay for gas. Food and water can be as cheap as I want to make it. Biking had also enlightened me to some of the more beautiful parts of life. There were times when the scenery became an unbelievable reality, like when every blade of grass was forest green and the sun beamed off the crinkling, autumn leaves. There were times when wind would hit my face ever so softly, heightening my senses but altogether separating me from actuality. Sensations like these reminded me why I majored in the fine arts, and how apparent it was that art imitates life when I take a minute to note the glorious world that I live in.

This thought process circulated my mind as we rode for Alex. We made a number of stops because my lower back continued to seize up. These stoppages were becoming a problem, and I was lost as to how to remedy my ailment. Fortunately, we only had to ride in the dark for about an hour, finally pulling into Alex around 9:00 p.m. There weren't many eating or drinking options at that time of night, even though we were in the downtown section of the city. We eventually settled on a small bar that was full of older, retired people. We didn't stay there long, mostly because we were tired and figured that going to a liquor store before they closed would be more beneficial to our wallets and overall health.

On our way to the hotel, it became obvious why Alex was considered such a tourist town. Even in the middle of the evening, the town had an aura that felt homey. It was no longer tourist season, so the scarce amount of people we saw roaming the sidewalks had to have been residents. We briefly chatted with a group of four older women, including one who had a large mole directly to the left of her nose.

"If you're looking for a party, you're in the wrong part of the city," said one of them. At that point, we knew our night was over.

We stopped at Target to buy a phone charger because I again forgot to pack one. After we arrived at the hotel I FaceTimed Stephanie, a recent love interest, but before I knew it, I was falling asleep while she talked about some subject that did not interest me.

* * *

The following morning started with me being able to return in a now inexplicably busted phone charger.

"Does it work?" asked the cashier.

"No, and I just bought it last night."

"Oh, well, that's okay. I can just credit the money back into your account." I smiled at her flirtatiously, but my gesture was unrequited.

Rhino and I stopped at a gas station next to the trail to buy some snacks, and then we jumped straight into riding. It wasn't as peaceful as the nighttime setting, but the vibe still had a relaxed feel to it. Physically, I felt much better than the previous night. My annoying lumbar had calmed down and I was able to ride to my standards.

Because I fell asleep early, I thought Rhino might be upset about missing out on a night of heavy drinking, but he was in a good frame of mind. We rode efficiently for a long stretch, not yet suffering any bodily malfunctions or annoyances.

We went back through Melrose, a city I knew of only because I had once been involved with a woman from there. After seeing where she lived, it explained some of her actions that had at one time irrationally bothered me.

When we neared St. Cloud, as if in homage to the season, we strode down Highway 23 in a blur. I'll never forget it. We just bullied our way home, running through stoplights and cutting off poor drivers who happened to be making right turns. I would see their right blinkers flashing, but I'd still go through. I couldn't help myself. I was emotionally unstable, albeit in a good way. I felt so invincible that even if a car hit me, I would just stand up, dust myself off, and keep going.

In this moment, all stress from my failed relationships was gone. All of Sammy's idiotic sentiments were so far from my consciousness. All my worries about having no money and what I was going to do after I graduated were gone. Even Rhino, who couldn't have been more than three feet away from me, felt so alien in that moment. I almost forgot he was with me.

We turned into the south side neighborhood still rolling. Together we burst through stop signs, feverishly calling out, "*Clear!*" at every red octagon. Once we pulled up the incline to our house, I was drained both physically and mentally. I sat on the steps to our door, reveling in the moment and embracing all the thoughts and emotions that were going through my brain.

I looked at Rhino. "There is no way this is can be our last ride of the year. That was too good."

It was a thoughtless statement, made entirely on raw emotion like many of my actions. Yet like those actions, it felt so right. It felt so right to lack clairvoyance, to think with my heart and not my brain. My life had been comprised of idiotic judgment for too long, but this stretch was also the most invigorating time of my life.

It was almost November. We weren't going to be able to go on any more trips. I didn't want the season to be over. I was like a little kid who was told he had to leave his friends and go home. I just wanted another trip. Just give me one more. One more chance to be free from social pressures and ridicule.

CHAPTER FIVE

I wouldn't get one more. Soon snow was falling and biking was merely a faint memory. Rhino and I had plenty to be proud of. The trips we took was something I never imagined doing in my life, much less in a two-month span.

When winter mercilessly arrived, there were other things I had to do to occupy my time. My relationship with Stephanie had evolved. We were not "together," but we spent a lot of time with each other, and she was someone I envisioned having a future with. She made the fast life seem so pointless. When I was with her, everything was right in my world.

After a month, our relationship quickly disintegrated. One evening, we had planned a double date with her friend and Rhino. I saw this as a step in our relationship. That afternoon, I awoke from a nap to go to class. I rolled over to check my phone, and upon seeing a text message from Stephanie, my life would never be the same.

Stephanie told me that she had sex with her ex-boyfriend, someone she consistently reassured me was no longer a part of her life. The news devastated me. Like a zombie, I walked to class and spent the whole session quietly staring at my professor, not in tune to his lecture at all.

"What did you think of that scene, Quentin?" asked my professor.

Without responding, I came back to reality, unable to mutter even a few coherent words. "I . . . uh . . . sorry, I must have missed that one, professor."

I was always a good student and I think my professor took pity on me when he saw my response. I walked out of class feeling worthless. I decided to skip my night class and instead get really drunk with Rhino and Mason. We went to the liquor store and bought a monster bottle of Grey Goose.

That night I got as drunk as I've ever been. Stephanie reached out to me a few times, but wisely, I didn't bother to engage her. I don't remember much, except that I woke up in the middle of the night with my head violently spinning. I tried to make it to the bathroom but couldn't even get out of my own room. I woke up the next morning face first in regurgitated Grey Goose.

For as awful as I felt the next morning, I needed that night to happen. I would see Stephanie again, her ability to lure me with sex was ever so uncanny. I didn't like her anymore. I hated her for what she did to me, but the animal urge inside me was too much to completely erase her from my life.

We would still hook up, which was almost always initiated by her drunkenly texting me. "Are you awake?" the text usually read. Like one of Pavlov's dogs, I instantly became her object. She could do whatever she wanted with me.

"Let's go take a shower," she said one time. While what ensued was erotically pleasing, it didn't make me any happier. I spent the next day cleaning out that same shower after my roommates collectively agreed that they wouldn't use it until I had cleaned the whole thing out. I assumed it was jealousy, or maybe they were trying to warn me.

With Stephanie, it didn't matter that I'd wake up later and hate myself for letting her use me. I suppose I was using her, but she wasn't going to be one of those women in my life; at least that's what I thought for the longest time. It's so cliché but so true that sex always complicates things. In this case, I didn't know who was being more complicated.

* * *

For a cyclist, the winter months are boring. A biker is very limited on what he or she can do. I stayed in decent biking shape, riding one or two times a week at the school gym. It was hard to find motivation to ride when I knew I wasn't going to be able to do anything serious for a number of months.

It was around Christmas that Rhino came up with a trip that would forever change our lives. We were in the kitchen having some beers when he blurted, "Why don't we go to Canada?"

Initially, I balked because I didn't want to wait until the summer to go on another trip.

"No, why don't we go to Canada over spring break?" I sat there for a moment, dumbfounded but more buzzed from the cheap beer.

"Where in Canada?" I asked.

"Winnipeg. It's only seventy miles from the border." In my head I thought this was the craziest idea ever.

I quietly responded, "I think that's doable."

Rhino had been to Canada once before on vacation but never to Winnipeg. Personally, I didn't care where we went. I just wanted to ride somewhere I knew would be a tough stretch and challenge us for all we were worth. When it came to the dates, we both agreed that spring break had to be it. Initially, I thought we might be too overzealous because of the weather, but as we started to plan the trip, the more it became realistic. We would need a large amount of luck, but historically, March had always been a hit or miss with the weather.

I broke the news to my parents on Christmas Eve, in the kitchen while my mom was making dinner.

"So Rhino and I are going to go to Canada over spring break."

My mom barely stopped seasoning her infamous pork chops. "Well, that's nice, Quentin."

I continued. "Yeah, we are going to bike there."

My dad put down his newspaper. "That is an absolutely horrible idea. No, you can't do that."

"Look, Dad, you can either support this decision or not, but it's happening."

Usually when I speak that brashly, my dad proceeds to yell or threaten me. This time he simply sat back and took it all in. It was as if he no longer felt like being a father, opting to be a friend instead.

* * *

This trip required the most preparation and effort I have ever devoted to something. We talked to many people who had ridden in the winter, albeit much shorter distances. Specifically Brody, an employee at Scheels, was the most helpful to our cause. He enlightened us that it would be smart to purchase a trailer to rotate carrying our supplies, thus allowing us to keep weight off our backs and at least one of our bikes.

"It's just the most practical way of going about it, although it might be the only practical thing about your trip," he said.

As time passed, the common sentiment among people I talked to was that they admired the ambition we had, but that the trip would be much more feasible in the warmer months. I don't know if people thought I had half a brain when they'd share this notion. Obviously it would make more sense to travel when the climate was in our favor, but there was not as much thrill or danger in that. Going to Winnipeg wasn't about taking the easiest, most pragmatic route. We were going for something legendary and emblematic of how we wanted to live.

The message Rhino and I had relayed to each other all along was "Do it for the boys." "The boys" were our roommates: Colin, Scooter, Mason, and Pinky. The phrase wasn't invented solely for our bike trip. It stemmed from a thought we believed in for all walks of life, whether it was going to introduce your friend to the random girl at the bar or if you needed to pick up Chipotle for your boy who was too lazy to leave the house. Doing it for the boys was about solidarity. Rhino and I were only part of the equation, but if our past rides taught us anything, it was that we were willing to do anything for our boys.

* * *

Two months before departure, we sat down on a Saturday and agreed not to leave the kitchen until we had our route mapped out. This signaled the sincerity of our trip and gave us more of a plan moving forward. The numbers lined up near perfect: going from St. Cloud, Minnesota, to Winnipeg would be 796 miles, or more romantically, 800 miles. Four hundred going there and four hundred back. To complete it by using all our spring break, it boiled down to approximately one hundred miles per day, adjusted for overnight stopping points.

Our first day was to be spent in Pine River, a city that was a half hour drive from Brainerd. With Rhino and I having ridden to Brainerd before, we expected this to be our easiest day of the trip since our bodies would be at full strength.

Clearbrook was where day two would culminate. Ideally, we would take the Paul Bunyan Trail most of the ride there, but with the weather being what it was, there was no way that the trail would be properly plowed and workable. Consequently, we would be relegated to riding on the shoulder of the road.

Our final night in Minnesota was to be spent in Karlstad, a mere thirty miles from the international border. We were fortunate Google Maps showed a hotel this close to the border. Thief River Falls was commonly thought to be the last stop that far north, but that would have killed our itinerary and put us in a precarious position if we had stopped there instead of going further north to Karlstad.

Day four would then be all about getting into Canada and making our way to the show, Winnipeg.

We had our plan, and now, for me, it was about getting into the best shape of my life. I ramped up my workouts. As often as I could, I would go for the most grueling rides possible at the gym, cranking up the resistance and getting my legs ready for a long, arduous haul. I also continued to drill my core, another part of the body a rider needs when performing at a high level to allow for consistent drive and a stable base.

It was tough walking to the gym in the cold months. There were days I didn't want to go because I was tired, lazy, or had homework. It was my last semester of college, and fortunately, I only had two classes, so my time devotion to that was much less than in previous semesters. I had to watch what I was eating and how frequently I consumed alcohol. I wasn't trying to become Lance Armstrong, but I also couldn't expect to complete this trip by consistently eating McDonalds and drinking Mountain Dew. It was a struggle because there were nights I wanted to go out and party with my boys. Like anything in life, I had to make sacrifices for the things I wanted and the people I cared about.

One day I had an idea about promoting our trip. I never thought that it would be something we would try to gain notoriety for, but the more I thought on it, the more it was clear that this was something unprecedented and highly difficult. People surely would find this story interesting, and after talking with Rhino, we wanted to capitalize on it.

I first went to my friend Tim, who had his own blog. He mostly wrote about basketball, but I knew him from an English class the previous summer and thought he would be a good source to break our story through. He had a fair amount of readers, so giving him the first opportunity for our story made sense. I messaged Tim and we set up a meeting on campus. We met with him in the coffee shop next to the library on campus. As expected, he thought the story was unique and loved the idea.

"Where did you get this idea?" asked Tim to no one in particular.

"That would definitely be Rhino, Tim. It was all him from the start." I said.

We all took turns speaking and asking questions. Rhino was not one for the spotlight, so his responses were brief and to the point. When pressed further on how he thought of going to Winnipeg, Rhino replied, "It seemed like the warmest place we could go."

I tried to be as open and honest as I could. Essentially, I felt it was my job to make this story go viral.

"Tim, I think there is a real art to what we are doing. What I mean by that is we are going to a place no one would expect. While everyone goes south for their break, we are going north." This was the simplest way to put it. We were doing the polar opposite of what everyone else was doing. Summing up our decision in this manner seemed like the best way to get people to understand.

We concluded our chat with Tim saying the article would be up in a week or so. That weekend, Tim contacted me over Facebook to clarify some details, and an hour later, I was reading his article while sitting in a bar near my cabin with my parents. It was a nice experience and something I never expected to do.

Unfortunately, Tim's article didn't give us the exposure I thought it would. I think people were skeptical and didn't think that Rhino and I would follow through. I had to think bigger. Tim's article was great, but people needed to see that what we were doing was unprecedented. I had to become more aggressive and search for bigger outlets to hear our story.

I contacted Dave Deland at the *St. Cloud Times* because he was their local beat writer. Fortunately, he had interest in what we were doing. It took some time to get an interview, but that was mostly because he wanted to promote us at the right time. As he said, "Too soon and people forget about your trip. Too late and there isn't enough time to tune people in."

Rhino and I met with Dave at the Caribou Coffee on campus. Dave walked in and I hailed him over from a table near the window. He was a tall, graying man. He was also extremely nice, and like Tim, shared in our enthusiasm for the trip. His recorder was an app on his iPhone, signaling to me he was a true professional.

As was the case with Tim, I did most of the talking. Rhino had a few things to say, mostly about how biking had been ingrained in him ever since he was a young boy. We talked logistics, challenges we expected to encounter, and things we wanted to see.

"The biggest thing, Dave," I began, "is that we aren't doing this for anyone other than ourselves. It may seem like this is half journey and half publicity stunt, but we have experience doing these trips. Now this will be our most challenging ride to date, but I see no reason why we can't do this thing."

I had to be confident in speaking to Dave. If I came off as unsure of how the trip would go, that would reflect in his story.

Overall the interview was fun, like it should be. Dave was here for a story, and he knew he had one. The interview neared completion. Dave told us that it would run in a section of the *Times* the following Tuesday. That was exciting because it meant we would be in the newspaper. I felt accomplished for being interviewed by someone of Dave's status, and it wasn't that hard to secure an interview. I simply e-mailed him and he found our story appealing. The experience with Dave taught me that I have to be aggressive and go for the things I want in life. As my mom always said, "The worst thing someone can say is no."

* * *

Days later, Rhino and I had our first test run in the frigid conditions. We had to get out of the gym and get acclimated to what the elements would be like. We were going out no matter what. There was no "weather permitting" on this ride. We didn't have anything special planned. It was to be our usual venture around the St. Cloud area. We layered up. Rhino had on long johns for both his legs and arms.

"Where did you get that?" I asked, laughing to myself.

"My dad gave them to me. Are you dumb?"

It was still February, and on this day, the wind was cold and bitter. After a mile of riding, my toes were starting to get cold. Rhino was in worse shape.

"I think my fingers are going to fall off," he cried.

We had to get out of the cold wind. We stopped at the Burger King in Sauk Rapids to warm up. When we walked in, people looked at us like we were deranged, homeless men. I couldn't stay there any longer. Rhino wanted to stay and recuperate, which irritated me because I didn't like being gawked at while in my arctic gear.

"We have to get out of here, dude. This place is tripping me out."

"Let's just stay awhile. I'm thinking of getting a burger anyway," said Rhino.

"Absolutely not. You are not getting a fucking burger. We came out here to ride. Now let's get back out there and do what we came to do."

"I want a burger."

My eyes became lasers. "Do you think we are going to be able to stop at a Burger King every time we get cold when we are on the *actual* trip? Hell no. We have to get out there and get used to this shit." Rhino acquiesced and we left.

In a few short miles, we had learned a lot already. It was apparent that wind was not going to be in our favor. We could only hope that for our trip the wind wouldn't be against us. We also had to invest in hand and toe warmers, plus any other items that would keep parts of the body that don't move during a ride from freezing.

* * *

It was getting closer to our departure date, and my nerves had ratcheted up since the test run. That ride assured me biking to Winnipeg wasn't going to be easy. We were no longer just riding one hundred miles per day. We would also be riding for our lives.

The next Tuesday came, and that morning, I went to a gas station to check out the *St. Cloud Times*. I anxiously began scrolling through the sections, but our story wasn't where Dave said it would be. I looked around the gas station to see if anyone was staring at me in my angst. I again checked through the whole paper but didn't find anything. I set the paper down to pick up my phone to contact Dave about a possible miscommunication.

As I picked up my phone, I looked down, and there it was. Dave told us to look for a section in the paper on our story. Instead, we were on the front page! My heart nearly exploded out of my chest. A smile so big you might have thought I won the lottery streamed across my face. I picked up all the papers out of the rack and brought them to the counter. The cashier looked at me like I was crazy, but when she made the connection, she simply smiled at me.

When I got back in my car, I called Rhino five times before he finally woke up and answered.

"Dude, get dressed. I have a surprise for you." I got back home and shoved the paper in his face. A boyish smile crept onto Rhino's face. "We have to go buy a ton of these," I said.

The front page was magnificent. Dave had sent a photographer over to our place after our interview to take pictures of us on our bikes. We didn't wear our gear for the photo op, only a few items that would enlighten people on our respective appearances.

Rhino and I took pictures of each other posing with a newspaper. I put a few of them on Facebook, and now the word was out. Dave had put us on the map with his article, and we were now validated.

I emailed Dave thanking him for his efforts, and we hopped in Rhino's car to make our way around the city. We stopped at a few Holiday gas stations, and the reactions were mostly the same. First, they wondered why we were buying so many newspapers, but their faces quickly turned to grins. It was at the Holiday in Sauk Rapids that I called my dad and told him of our story being on the front page.

"Dad, you're not going to believe this, but we are on the front page of the *St. Cloud Times*."

All he could say was congratulations, but I knew he was proud of me. As expected, he also reminded me how difficult the journey was going to be.

At another gas station, a younger looking clerk looked at the paper and then back at me.

"You're much cuter in person," she said, a smile emanating off her face.

Besides saying thank-you, I didn't know how to take her kind words because I was wearing sweatpants and a sweatshirt. I then went on Snapchat and did a lengthy number telling people to go buy a paper and check it out. The attention was beginning to pour in on Facebook. We were boasting, but we had to. A moment like this only lasts for so long.

I went to class that day feeling like a rock star. My professor walked near me and I calmly asked, "Hey, Dr. Simpson. Would you like to see something cool?"

She looked at me as if I might reveal to her a marijuana pipe. Her face was worried, but when I showed her the article, she lit up.

"Can I show the class?" she asked.

"Go ahead. I have plenty," I confidently replied.

There was now pressure on us. We couldn't fail because people had read about us and were anxiously tracking our journey. It was the first time in my life that I felt I had people counting on me. It wasn't like I couldn't walk around campus without being stopped, but the university had gotten behind us. People had taken notice.

The fine arts department had put the newspaper up in their office for all to see. MPR (Minneapolis Public Radio) wanted a piece of us. We agreed to do a phone interview with them when we got to Winnipeg. Doug Lunney from the *Winnipeg Sun* called Rhino, and we did an interview for his paper. At the conclusion of the interview, Rhino and I took a selfie to send to Doug. This photo would later be in one of the largest newspapers in Winnipeg.

The hype surrounding our trip was dominating my thoughts. I was very proud of us, but we hadn't done anything yet. We still had to go out and ride, which was what we had wanted to do all along. Paranoia set in and I began thinking of all the things that could go wrong. It would have felt horrible if something happened to prevent this trip from taking place. For days, I struggled with paranoia and euphoria. This was the most exciting time of my life, but it was also the most stressful. This was my chance to do something meaningful, a chance to chase my dreams.

* * *

The weekend before our most epic bicycle journey, we drove our route to Canada. There had been much debate about whether or not this tarnished some of the elegance of the trip. Scooter called it cheating. To us, it was strictly precautionary. We couldn't venture into low-population areas in the winter without knowing at least a little about what to expect.

We notified each hotel that we were coming, which turned out to be absolutely necessary because the one in Karlstad would not have had room if we didn't make reservations in advance.

It was also imperative because when we got to the border, we were hounded by the patrol stationed there. They didn't believe that we would be biking there.

"What are you trying to pull here?" asked the crabby middle-aged border guard.

"Nothing, sir. We are just traveling this route because next week we will be on our bikes going to Winnipeg," I calmly answered.

"You know it is going to be negative twenty next week, right?" said the sad man.

"Well, I was looking at the forecast and it said it was going to be about thirty out."

"Is that Fahrenheit or Celsius?"

I stumbled. "I'd assume Fahrenheit. All our temperatures are in that measurement."

The man looked at me, unable to determine how trustworthy I was. "Do you have any alcohol in the car?"

"I have half a bottle of vodka in the trunk. Is that okay?"

"Technically I'm not supposed to let you in if you have alcohol."

"Well, I mean I can throw it out if you want. It was just for tonight at the hotel." I turned to Rhino. He shrugged his shoulders as neither of us knew what to do. "Sir, I have copies of a newspaper detailing our trip if you want to see them. They're in the trunk as well."

"You know, I would like to see that."

I slowly got out of my car and went to the trunk. I opened it, revealing Rhino's bottle of New Amsterdam and a litany of newspapers.

"Here it is, sir," I said, handing him a copy.

He looked over the front page, but I was unable to decipher if he was reading or staring at the pictures. He looked up at me and then turned around to yell to his coworkers. "Damn, they are actually telling the truth. Okay, you guys can go through. You said you will be back next week?"

"Yep."

"Okay. Have fun, fellas."

I thanked the man and we continued on. The roads were absolutely horrible, to the extent that there was no shoulder lane to account for bicycles. We passed a few deserted towns and were then on a highway headed straight to Winnipeg. This would be the route we would have to take to Winnipeg, as deserted and potentially dangerous as it was.

After almost an hour of driving through empty cornfields and passing the occasional gas station, we arrived in Winnipeg, and the city was huge. We had come from seemingly nowhere and were now in the middle of a giant metropolis. Rhino had booked us a hotel before we went across the border, so we headed there. On our way, we passed stunning architecture, an art museum, a Target, and what seemed like thirty Tim Horton's, the Canadian version of Panera Bread.

After driving in circles looking for a parking spot, we settled into our hotel that was nestled in among the city. Rhino and I ventured out for dinner, walking along the main downtown strip. We stopped at a venue that had a lit-up sign. When we walked in, we found out it doubled as a pizza joint and nightclub, but few people were in at the time. I bought a few slices of pizza and a cider beer that was the best I've ever had.

"Where is everyone?" I asked the cute brunette who sliced up my pizza.

"It's spring break here, so no one is on campus."

"On campus?" I asked with a look of confusion.

"Well, yeah, you are on the University of Winnipeg campus."

Amazed, I walked back to Rhino and told him of our whereabouts. We didn't stay long because there weren't many people there. We walked back to our hotel, passing the same people we saw on our walk there.

The next morning, we had to leave early so that Rhino could get to work on time. We stopped at Tim Horton's for breakfast. As we drove out of the city, it became apparent that Winnipeg had seen better days. Much of the industry and architecture on the outskirts looked worn and ready to collapse. The only building that looked modern was IKEA. The drive out of Winnipeg and back to the border was again very dull and lifeless.

At the border, there were about ten blocks of cement to prevent cars from speeding through, but we encountered much less resistance from authorities. The most exciting part about driving home was listening to Mason and Rhino have a phone conversation regarding Mason's newest love interest, Macy.

"Hello. Mason, are you awake?" Rhino began.

"Yes. What do you want, fuck boy?"

"Tell me about this Macy I keep hearing about."

"Oh no," said Mason, exhausted. "I'm hungover. Let's talk about this some other time."

"No, now. I keep hearing her name but I've never met her."

"Ryan, don't worry about it. It's none of your business."

"But I have to know. If you don't tell me, then I'm going to have to go through other sources."

"Look, you do what you have to do, but I'm not talking about her."

At this point, Rhino decided to include my portion of the story. "Q tells me you guys almost dated last year and that you and Scooter almost had a threesome with her."

A pause ensued. "Goddamn it. Don't listen to anything he says. You know he is just going to tell the story so that it makes him look good."

"But Mason this story is about you. What's Macy's last name?"

"I'm not telling you."

"Mason. Q is telling me that her last name is Love. So are you dating Macy Love?"

"We are not talking about this!"

Rhino looked at his phone and realized Mason had hung up. At that point, he looked at me and the two of us burst into laughter. I envisioned Mason lying on the couch, groaning and trying to think of the best way to rid himself of a massive hangover and plotting revenge for my revelation. The sequence didn't last long, but it certainly helped with the monotony of the car ride.

CHAPTER SIX

We were now a few days away from leaving, and my anticipation was uncontrollably high. Reality was coming to fruition. When you plan a trip so far in advance and invest a lot of time, effort, and money into making it a reality, you wind up forgetting you're actually taking the trip. This is simply because you get so lost in planning that you forget about what it is that you're planning. This happened to me, and I became second fiddle to my own show.

Rhino texted me midway through the week and told me his dad was going to meet us on our first night in Pine River. This was a big deal because until then we had no secondary plans for if one of us got hurt or a bike broke down. The news eased some of the enormous stress that I had.

That week was also stressful from a safety perspective. I was mindful of everything I did, careful not to injure myself. I didn't participate in intramurals basketball or do any sort of training, save for one more outdoor ride to try to further acclimate to the weather.

During this ride, I stopped at Nicole's house, a woman I had been seeing for about a month. I whipped out my phone to call her and grew frustrated when it had frozen.

"Didn't you see me?" a female voice said.

I turned around and Nicole was right there.

"What timing! I was actually just about to call you, Nicole."

She buried her face and giggled. "I have good news for you."

"What's that?"

"I got my period."

I had mixed emotions. I had actually stopped by Nicole's house to see if she wanted to have a quick joining of body parts. "That's great, babe. I guess that means the condoms are working, right?"

"Right!"

"Nicole, I have to get going and finish my ride, but thank you for being in my life. This last month has been fantastic."

Nicole was a great woman. I thought the world of her. I would leave her voicemails so she would think I was different and romantic. The tactic worked, and I wanted to keep doing things like that for her.

After the Stephanie debacle, I figured it would be a long time before I met someone I liked again, so I reverted back to sleeping around. When I met Nicole, she brought joy back into my life.

For Valentine's Day, I took her to see the new film *Fifty Shades of Grey*. "I hoped you weren't taking me to that movie because you had some weird sex fetish," Nicole said as we laid in my bed that night after having sex. I had just turned on a playlist I made for her.

"No. That was not my intention at all. I didn't even want to go to that movie. I just figured you would like it."

"Do you think I'm that basic?" she asked, half joking and half curious.

I didn't think Nicole was basic at all. She was beginning to dominate my thoughts, which was a cathartic release from all the pressure surrounding our trip.

* * *

The night before we left, I was very emotional. My parents came up to meet Nicole, give me some supplies, and see me one last time before I left. We drove around St. Cloud and got lost on our way to dinner. I felt so alive on that night, with emotions running through my mind I had never before experienced. The beautiful nervousness validated what I was doing. As much as my parents wanted my dream to be accomplished, they also wanted me to be safe and to come home in one piece.

"Just be safe, and wear a condom if need be," were the constant themes uttered by my mother. Although with Nicole there, I don't know why she said that.

Later that night, I said good-bye to everyone. First, I said good-bye to my mom, who surely was sick to her stomach worrying. Then I said good-bye to my dad. Earlier that week, we planned for him to meet us in Winnipeg, so I knew I would be seeing him shortly. After my parents left, I said good-bye to Nicole.

"So this is it, huh?" I said.

"You better come back in one piece," she said.

"Oh, Nicole. Don't make me more anxious."

"But seriously, come back. I want to see you again."

Nicole actually changed my life from the moment I saw her. It was only a month or so prior in an English class. Since I was a film studies student, I didn't know many of the people who majored in English. I walked in the first day, nervous yet excited to take some different classes. I sat by the wall facing the rest of the class.

"How are you doing?" I said to my professor, the aforementioned Dr. Simpson.

She returned a look that suggested she knew me but couldn't remember how she knew me. I didn't tell her that I took a writing course with her the previous summer.

After our exchange, I looked to my right and saw a nice looking blonde woman. She was very pale. *Winter hasn't done her any favors*, I thought to myself. Yet she was a sight to behold. She reminded me of John Cusack's back-and-forth girlfriend in *High Fidelity*. For a moment I thought she might have been more rebellious, the type that would go to concerts and occasionally smoke marijuana.

Nothing happened between this angelic woman and I for the first few weeks of class. Then one day, I turned and she was staring at me. It was an extremely lustful gaze, and her look made me lose all train of thought. Once she knew I spotted her, she quickly looked away, but the event sparked my interest in her. After class, I went home and looked for her on Facebook. I added her, and a few hours later, we were "friends."

I wound up spending the majority of that night looking through her pictures, trying to get a sense of who she was without ever having talked to her. The behavior could have been considered creepy, but it was a representation of how enamored I was with her. I looked at many of her pictures and thought, *Man, it would be nice to be in this woman's life.*

Soon after that day, I matched with her on Tinder, a dating app for phones. Normally, I would have sent her a message as soon as we matched, but this time I tried something different and decided on approaching her in person the next day.

That class period, I was a bundle of nerves. I nervously looked at the clock any chance I got. I pondered my approach and what I would say to her. It was simultaneously the most fun and least productive class period I've ever participated in. When 2:40 p.m. came, it was time to make my move.

I stood up from my chair and hurriedly yet cautiously made my way to where she was sitting. She was putting on her jacket when I asked, "Hey, Nicole. How are you doing?"

She looked at me then put her head down to continue packing up her things.

"I'm doing well."

"Where are you off to?" I asked as we made our way out of the classroom.

"I'm going to Caribou before my next class."

"Ah, I see. Do you want to get a coffee or something?"

"Um, I already have one," she said.

I had made the critical mistake of failing to notice she already had a cup of coffee in her hand. Mentally, I became flummoxed, unsure of what to say to save face. "Oh, my mistake."

"We can still hang out, if you want," she said in an uninterested tone.

"That sounds fun. I have nothing going on."

We sat down at a table and made awkward small talk, a common occurrence on first dates, if I could even call what we were doing a first date. We talked about an array of topics, but nothing extremely notable. The entire time, I got the impression that she felt obligated to sit down and talk with me rather than her actually wanting to hang out. Things were made more awkward when my friend Jeff showed up.

"Hey, hey. You two know each other?" Jeff said.

I froze. Jeff and I had hung out a fair amount the previous summer, doing many things that single guys did. The fact that he knew Nicole scared me. *Had they been together?* was the pervading thought flowing inside of my head. Nicole greeted him, and I hoped that he would not be joining us at the table. Fortunately, he left shortly after, and I was not forced to endure a painfully awkward three-way chat.

"Do you know that guy?" I asked Nicole.

"Yeah. He hangs out in Caribou all the time."

The topic didn't linger much longer. I thought they might have been involved, but I didn't care. Jeff was my friend, and I was hoping that Nicole would be my girlfriend. The past was the past. Hopefully she was my future.

My quasi-date with Nicole abruptly ended when she stood up. "So I have to go to class."

"Oh. Yeah, no, I totally understand. This was nice, Nicole."

"Yeah, it was," she said without much conviction.

When she left, I thought that was the last time we would talk. My hopes were dashed. Her departure insinuated that she wasn't interested. I was fine though because I knew I saw the opportunity through and could go to sleep at night knowing I tried.

The night before I left, Nicole and I kissed each other good-bye, and then she left into the night. I desperately hoped she wouldn't become only a memory, and that I would see her again. We weren't at the "I love you" stage yet, but I really hoped I would be able to see her again, above anyone else. I was only going to be gone for ten days, but it felt like I was about to embark on something I wasn't going to return from.

As much as Rhino and I planned for this, we also didn't truly know what we could expect. What if a bear came out of the woods and attacked us? What if rabid dogs bit into Rhino's leg? What if my bike completely broke? It was all conjecture but all possible.

CHAPTER SEVEN

The next morning, I woke up. The calendar read March 6, 2015. Rhino and I agreed to wake up at 7:00 a.m., ready to embark on our journey. We said good-bye to Scooter and Pinky, who had risen early to see us out, but not before they gave us an expected hard time.

"You better do this whole trip. No pussying out. I'm serious," warned Scooter.

"Scooter, chill," I said, thrown off at his early morning rage.

We walked our bikes out the front door and onto Eighth Street. Scooter took a picture for Facebook and then we left, not knowing what the future held.

We began our journey through the neighborhood where all our friends resided, taking a left and moving down Fifth Avenue, parallel to the university. I was set to carry all our gear in a trailer, just like Brody had recommended. Rhino would take it the next day, and we planned to keep rotating throughout the trip. It was dead outside because no one was on campus.

"Not exactly the send-off I was hoping for," I said to Rhino, half joking.

We crossed over Highway 23, passing all the bars that had been so good to me during my time in St. Cloud. We turned right and headed for the back roads just outside of town.

We didn't make it out of St Cloud before Rhino noticed he had forgot his phone. "Do we turn around?" he asked.

"I don't think that's possible in all honesty, man. Time is of the essence."

It wasn't the end of the world, but we were a few miles in and turning around felt wrong. This decision created an issue because now we only had one phone in case of emergency. The problem with this was that Bruce (Rhino's dad) had no idea Rhino had forgotten his phone. The only saving grace was that Rhino had Bruce's number memorized. It was perhaps the most dysfunctional start to a ride imaginable. It was also everything we tried to avoid during our planning stages. It was another reminder that things never go according to plan.

We stopped a few miles later and I fished for my phone, which turned out to be frozen and out of commission. This happened on many practice runs, but I wasn't expecting it to happen already. I knew my phone wouldn't become functional until it warmed back up.

Unsurprisingly, it's a difficult task to warm up a phone when on the back roads of northern Minnesota and stops are at a premium. Not even twenty miles in, we were already encountering glaring problems.

Still, there was nothing we could do. We continued on, getting twenty miles in before we took our first stretching break. My goggles had fogged up to the point where I could barely see. I was overheated from all the layers I was wearing, but it beat the alternative. We weren't riding at a poor pace, but we still had roughly eighty miles to go.

The trailer I was carrying began to make life difficult. The wind only added to the resistance I was feeling with each turn of the pedal. Climbing hills with the trailer dragging behind me took the most energy. When I was on flat ground, the trailer actually boosted my speed, but as soon as an incline approached, it was twice as difficult to get that momentum back in my favor.

I wasn't planning on needing too much water until we hit Freedham, where they had the convenience store we stopped at on our initial ride to Brainerd. I only had two bottles of water with me at the time, and one of them froze. The other one I thought had frozen, but at one stop, nearing dehydration, I opened the lid and discovered ice had only blocked the top of the mug. I drank the little water that wasn't frozen, and it was becoming obvious that we needed to get to Freedham soon. Getting there proved to be challenging. We mapped out more back roads on our drive the previous week. To avoid gravel roads, we wound up putting ten extra miles on our ride. That meant while we had biked forty miles, we only progressed about thirty miles forward. It was something we expected, but didn't mentally prepare for the strain it would cause on our attitudes.

Things at this juncture were not looking well. We thought that it would be possible to be in Brainerd by 1:00 or 2:00 p.m., but the weather was forcing us to adjust our goals. It was noon and we were not yet to Freedham.

"Goddamn, this fucking wind," I barked to Rhino.

He was munching on an off brand toaster pastry when he looked up at me. "It's a bitter battle."

"No shit. And this stupid trailer isn't helping. I feel like I'm carrying a passed out Mason on the back."

When I looked at my watch, I became irate. What started out as a journey for the ages was quickly becoming even more grueling than originally anticipated. By the time we finally got to Freedham, I told Rhino that we would have to adjust our goals.

"There is no way we are going to make it to Pine River at this pace," I said.

"We just have to keep grinding," replied Rhino.

"Well, duh. It's easy for you to say. You don't have this trailer. You are definitely taking it tomorrow."

Rhino nodded his head in a way that suggested he definitely did not want to take the trailer. I was in better shape than he was, so it made sense for me to take it. I wasn't upset with him. I only wanted the wind to let up and give us a chance. We were riding as well as we could, but traversing across Minnesota in March via bicycle began to seem foolish. We walked into the same convenience store and were right away met with weird looks from the two people in the store. One of them was the owner of the store we had previously met on our initial way back from Brainerd. He was a middle-aged man with a long beard. The other wore glasses and made sure I knew he thought I looked odd. I told the owner about our trip.

"You guys are a ways away from Pine River, I'm afraid," said the owner.

"That's true, but we will be all right," I said back, trying to hide my concern.

"Getting to Pine Rive might be hard today," the owner continued.

"Yeah, but we have no other option. Rhino here forgot his phone, so our safety net has no idea where we are."

His place didn't accept credit cards, so I had to borrow cash from Rhino, which angered him because he had very little to begin. My phone finally turned on and Rhino left Bruce a message.

We got back outside, looked at each other, and then jumped back into grind mode. The break ended up benefitting us. We mentally reset, putting our little spat behind us. The ride was still difficult. It was practically unfair. The wind was killing us, and there was no indicator it would relent soon.

I began to think about how our situation would affect our social standing. It was the first day and already we had fallen behind schedule. People would think we were jokers, unable to complete what we had came out to do. I wasn't content with that feeling. The frustration continued to anger me, conjunctively fueling my legs to push harder.

Since we traveled virtually the same route before, we knew when to expect certain landmarks. This time I didn't see the ostrich house, but I did see a construction crew working on a displaced power line. The crew was on a bend, and I remembered this point. I knew Brainerd was on the horizon.

As we continued to ride, I didn't see anything else that looked familiar. It was during this stretch that dogs became troublesome. The first encounter involved a bigger dog that slowly barked and made its way into the road. It was not going to harm us as long as we kept our heads down and proceeded forward.

The next run in was much more perilous. This time Rhino was about twenty feet in front of me. I saw a large dog and a very small one came bursting out of a yard on the left. They were both following him for a couple hundred feet, despite the pleas of an old woman.

"Come back, you damn dogs!" was her only attempt at mitigating their chase.

I wanted to start laughing but then I heard a large vehicle behind me begin to slam on its brakes. It was a semi and it passed me and then fully slammed on its brakes to avoid hitting the dogs. I turned back and saw the fat, old woman now in the road still hollering. The semi slowly moved forward, and I saw that Rhino was unscathed. It was becoming clear that we had to get off the road because cars were not expecting us. The next time a car slammed on its brakes, we might not get so lucky.

Brainerd finally arrived. We were at the city limits on the outskirts of town when a truck narrowly avoided hitting me. I looked down and saw that I was on the shoulder and that the person in the truck was just being an asshole. When I looked back up Rhino was wagging his middle finger at the truck. I assumed he too almost got hit.

The truck then braked and turned around in the middle of the road. My head began to race as I ran through all possible scenarios. Rhino continued to flick the driver off. When the driver rolled down his window, the face of a middle-aged man with only half a set of teeth appeared. Driving slowly, our eyes met and I swiveled my head to maintain eye contact. When he passed, I noticed a shotgun racked on his rear window. My heart rate continued to spike as I thought of the possibilities. Rhino and I continued our pace and the weird man fortunately did not reappear.

Getting through Brainerd was a hassle, considering I had the trailer on my rear. Cars had to swerve out of the way to avoid clipping my back end. Rhino cut me off near a pizzeria, which automatically made my blood boil. I knew it was unintentional, but the way he did it irked me.

"Watch where you're fucking going!" I yelled.

He smiled, suggesting that he did it on purpose. In the moment, I was angered, but I knew he was only trying to motivate me. Annoyingly, it was now around dinnertime. I was so hungry I could have ate Rhino's proverbial "ass end of a boar pig." All we ate the whole day were toaster pastries and granola bars. A medium-rare prime rib sounded like the perfect remedy to my long day.

Five miles later, as we merged onto the highway, we stopped at the 371 Diner. We still had a ways until we would reach Pine River, but it was time to unwind and think about our next move.

The diner was a total throwback to the days when roller skates and striped shirts were popular. Sitting down, people were looking at me like I had "self-made" tattooed on my forehead. In their defense, I looked like I had just climbed out of the nearby woods.

With the sun beginning its descent, decisions had to be made. I opted for the cheese fries and cottage cheese to go along with my burger. Rhino had applesauce. The reality was we had made it seventy-five miles, yet still had another thirty to go. I knew that wasn't going to happen as I looked outside and saw the sun fast descending. Clearly, we overestimated the swiftness with which we would be able to travel in these conditions.

"I think we should call Bruce," I said as I looked at my phone that was plugged into the wall. "It really is our only option at this point."

"We could try for at least half the miles. We would only be riding in the dark for a little bit then," Rhino said, clearly disappointed with how the day had went.

"Could do, but honestly, dude, we need to start thinking about tomorrow. I mean, we are out here on vacation essentially. We have nothing to be sorry about. We busted our asses today. Fuck the wind. If we call Bruce and get a lift, I don't think we cheated anyone today."

Rhino looked at me in agreement. "Fine. Let's do it. Give me your phone."

Bruce soon arrived to pick us up. This was my first dalliance with Bruce. I don't know if he thought we would be in great spirits or not, but Bruce brought an interesting vibe to the group. He pestered us.

"When I didn't hear from you guys, I thought you had turned around and called it quits. I was just going to go back home," he said.

"No, Bruce. Rhino forgot his phone. We put our heads down the whole day. Miles and miles of wind. Too hard to stop for long periods," I said, exasperated.

Bruce was not the most agile, so we had to do all the work getting our bikes into the trunk. Being pretty tired, the last thing I wanted to do was try to maneuver our bikes into the back of his SUV. I thought he might do it for us, but once I saw his physical condition, I knew that wasn't happening.

Bruce wrongfully assumed we were novices attempting to do the unthinkable before we had even considered the thinkable. Since Rhino had not enlightened him on our previous journeys, he haggled us as if it were our first time riding bicycles.

"You guys didn't get very far today."

"Dad, the wind is terrible!" said Rhino angrily.

"Yeah, Bruce, there wasn't a whole lot we could do," I chimed while rushing to our defense.

"Yeah, but still. Back in my day, I used to ride forty miles a day to work. And I had to ride over this hill that was two miles high."

From the backseat, I looked at Rhino to see if Bruce was hyperbolizing. "True story," Bruce continued. "Oh, man. That was a battle. Every single day too."

Bruce's heckling made me want to ride better. I already wanted it to be tomorrow so that I could go right back out there and prove that I had what it took for this trip. I decided that when I was feeling sore in the thighs or lower back, I would think of how much I hated the fact that Bruce was maligning our epic ride. Similar to a cat chasing a string, I envisioned a portrait of him hanging in front of me and me pedaling harder and harder just to grab the said portrait; only when I finally grabbed the photo, I would punch a hole in it.

We pulled in to the Rodeway Inn on the outskirts of Pine River. We stayed at the Rodeway in Brainerd back in the fall, so we knew the rooms were going to be horrendous. Then again, all we wanted was a room.

The woman working the counter when we drove through was there, albeit this time friendlier. The first time I talked to her, she was very disinterested in our trip and even the fact that we wanted to stay at her motel.

"Um, I might have some rooms available, but no promises" was the phrase she uttered when I politely asked her about availability.

Since there were only two other cars outside, I knew she was just being difficult the previous week. Judging by her build and attitude, I think she would have preferred turning on late night television and chomping down a plate full of nachos instead of getting us situated.

After settling in to our disgusting room, Rhino and I drove to a nearby gas station and picked up some food. When we came back, Rhino and I spoke very little, instead opting to let the TV do the talking. I fell asleep shortly thereafter, pondering how I could make the next day better.

CHAPTER EIGHT

When I woke up the next morning, it was still dark out. We wanted to beat the morning rush, if Pine River even had one. I thought Rhino might take his time getting ready, but the whole half hour we allotted to preparing for the day was done very economically. Physically, I was feeling ready to go, a byproduct of training during those long winter months. A few minutes of light stretching and munching down some Oreos righted my attitude and had me pumped to get back on the road. Yesterday was yesterday, and today was today.

We started off very smooth. We got to Backus, which was ten miles away, in an hour. Rhino stopped for a beef stick and some stretching.

"Slim Jims always put my mind right," Rhino noted.

We were very happy with our progress and thought that luck might be more on our side today. What ensued after those early ten miles was, unfortunately, hellacious.

The wind broke through the morning calmness and was once again right in our faces. Hackensack, the next city, was only seven miles from Backus, but that distance felt like forever. By now neither of us had the trailer because Bruce threw it in his trunk, but climbing over hills was still a nightmare. It was on this stretch to Hackensack that I began to think in binaries. I started to appreciate the hills and the wind, even though they nearly broke me.

"Oh yeah, I like this," I continued to say to myself. "Give me more. Give me more."

I had no other option. I could either let nature win, or I could take what she gave me and embrace it. I no longer tried to get over the hills quickly. Instead, I took a calm and steady approach. This approach didn't make me go any faster, but it did put my mind at ease, which was so critical in those conditions.

The small town of Hackensack came into view. We weren't interested in stopping because we were already falling behind our itinerary. We passed a speed-reader designed for cars. The number eight popped up, further reminding us just how slow we were riding.

Hackensack wasn't totally foreign to me. Nicole worked at a summer camp in Hackensack called Deep Portage. There was also a place called Kensack Karpets, and Nicole never knew why it was entitled that. To many, the Kensack abbreviation was obvious, but to her it was mystifying. Riding through Hackensack reminded me of her and what I left behind in St. Cloud.

We proceeded onward toward Walker, another fifteen miles ahead. To get there, we continued our march up some of the roughest hills imaginable. Cars would pass, and every time I tilted my head to the left, I could see a look of disbelief on the passenger's faces, as if they couldn't fathom what they were viewing.

Their looks made me ask myself: *What else would I rather be doing?* I couldn't come up with an answer. I didn't fully grasp the concept, but I was happy in my seemingly miserable state. As much as these hills were a pain, I again was beginning to appreciate them. Rhino and I always said, "What goes up, must come down," and this was no different. The day was gloomy and there was no sun to keep us warm. The wind howled and barked, but it did not deter us. It reminded me of the film *300*. Nature was doing everything it could to make us quit, but we just wouldn't relent. We wanted this so bad. It was our time.

We were a few miles outside of Walker when we approached a casino. It was similar to one of those smoky, rundown places that old people flocked to because they had nothing else to do. It brought me back to when I turned eighteen years old and went to Mystic Lake Casino almost every day. It was a complete waste of time and money, but I did it because I couldn't find something better to do. It was then that I realized I had no moral high ground over the people in that casino because I used to be just like them.

As we turned left and away from the casino at the first stoplight in what seemed like days, a frozen lake came into view. I imagined what this place would look like in the summer, with boats cruising by, cars constantly on the road, and a general sense of content.

But right now, there was no visual satisfaction to be had. Instead, the lake was frozen and powder white engulfed the whole body of water.

As mentioned, we initially desired to jump on the Paul Bunyan Trail. Google Maps had it mapped out at around 100 miles for the day if we took that trail. Unfortunately, snow dominated the pathway, which meant that we had to ride parallel to the trail on the road. What we later learned was that this would force us to travel an extra fifteen miles. This meant our goal that day changed from 100 miles to about 115 miles. Essentially, tacking on fifteen miles to an already grueling 100 miles was a slap in the face. It's comparable to finishing a multiple-choice exam, only to be told that there is an additional essay portion once you are about to hand in your exam.

We finally made it to Walker, meeting up with Bruce in the downtown sector of the city. We had to get something to eat. It was already around 1:00 p.m., so we were behind on lunch. We couldn't decide where to eat.

"You guys go find a place and call me. I don't want to be walking around in this cold," Bruce said from the comforts of his Chevy.

Rhino and I walked into a coffee house. Instantly we were greeted with odd looks from both the patrons and employees. In fact, none of the employees even bothered to say hello. There was a group of women having what looked like a bachelorette party, and they too stared, appalled that us two homeless-looking men would wander into a coffee house.

"Let's leave," I said to Rhino. "I don't feel wanted here."

"Well, let's just see what they have to eat," he replied.

"No. We are leaving, dude." I walked out ashamed and pretending I didn't just try to eat there.

We settled on a local diner that only served breakfast. Our waitress could not have cared less that we were there.

"Can I take your order?" she said in an unwelcoming tone.

Since the establishment was soon closing, she probably just wanted to go home. Instead, she was going to have to serve us three raggedy-looking men. She was an attractive woman, close to our age but with the patience and attitude of a thirteen-year-old girl. Every so often, I run into a server like the one we had on this day. I couldn't understand why she was so opposed to us being there. It wasn't like we were ordering diet waters and asking her what time her shift ended. I chalked it up to being in Walker, on a day so cold a yeti would seek shelter.

Bruce, as expected, wouldn't quit with the insults. "You guys are going too slow. You need to pick up the pace, damn it. You still have sixty miles until Clearbrook."

"We are giving it all we can, Bruce. That shit out there is *brutal*." I squealed.

"Well, yeah, I know, but you guys are going to be riding all night at this pace," said Bruce in a condescending manner.

I looked at Bruce sternly, dumbfounded that he thought we were taking our sweet, old time. Bruce just sat there, chewing his hash browns with his mouth open, revealing a set of teeth that needed a professional cleaning.

We finished our meals and were ready to hit the road again. Rhino inexplicably had to use the restroom, apparently forgetting that we were just in a restaurant, so we stopped at a Holiday gas station.

"You're putting us behind schedule," I said to him as he came out, as payback for him cutting me off the previous day.

Bemidji was our next stop. It was only thirty miles away, but it was a difficult thirty miles. Climbing hills was to be expected, but this was downright sadistic of Mother Nature. The wind from the surrounding lakes was rattling me to the bones. Gaining any sort of traction or momentum was impossible. We were grinding. All we could do was put our heads down and ride it out.

We arrived in Cass Lake, a city I later learned was the site of an American Indian reservation. Even though we had recently eaten lunch, I was starving. We stopped at a gas station, knowing Bemidji was still about fifteen miles away. Just after the gas station was a highway where we would take a left, meaning the torrential wind was now going to be our best friend, or our continued enemy.

Outside the gas station, I noticed an elderly woman sitting on the ground, showing no interest in glancing our way. She was of American Indian descent, and she just sat there. She wasn't waiting for anyone. She was just waiting for the time to pass. I admired her for braving the elements, but I was more captivated knowing she had a story. I wasn't going to ask her to tell me her life story, but knowing she had one gave me a weird feeling of satisfaction.

I went inside and bought a breakfast burrito and a Nestlé chocolate milk. I figured this would last me until Bemidji. I had only budgeted so much money for the trip, and already I was beginning to think that I would have to turn to my credit card in a few days.

Rhino and I ate silently, looking at each other if only to marvel the presence of each other. We didn't get to talk a whole lot. In all honesty, the trip wasn't going as planned, and we didn't know who to blame. I love Rhino. I could never question his heart or ability to persevere under less than ideal circumstances. But since he was the person I spent literally all my waking hours with, he was going to be the one who I would moan and groan at, even if he had no complicity in my frustration.

"Look," I started, "if we can just get to Bemidji, then we can start thinking about tomorrow. I at least want to get those miles in. After that, I don't see a destination that is close enough to get to."

Rhino didn't scoff at this idea. Internally, he felt like I did: disappointed that all the hard work and sacrifice we made wasn't enough. It brought me back to the ninth grade, where in science class, Mr. Mullin had a photo of a crying football player that read, "When your best isn't good enough."

It was then that I realized life is too short to be upset about numbers and goals. What we were doing still made me feel alive and fulfilled. Rhino couldn't control the elements. I couldn't control his dad's diction. We could only control our attitudes.

"Let's get back out there," I said, standing up from the curb and hopping on my bike. "There is no place I'd rather be."

We carried on, hopping on the highway with Bemidji all but guaranteed to be our last stop of the day because of the sun's imminent descent. I began to realize that the worst part about the wind was that it eliminated any potential conversation I could have with Rhino. On the highway, this reality was even more exacerbated. I was with him, but I was never *with* him. We couldn't lean on each other for emotional support. He was just a physical being that was next, behind, or in front of me while I powered through the most physically demanding trip of my life.

As we trudged further toward Bemidji, the sun was falling faster than Newton's apple. Cars driving at speeds eighty miles per hour and more whizzed past us. At times it was comforting. At other moments, I would hear a semi hit the brakes or switch lanes and my heart rate would spike. Even when the semi passed safely, it always hampered my pace because the wind the semi generated would blow me to the side. I became an object that got caught in the wind, but it trumped being Stephanie's object of desire.

With the sun all but gone, signs for Bemidji approached. All told, we needed around 115 miles, and we were at 70. The previous day, we came up 25 miles short. That was respectable because we had hammered out 75. On this day, we were five miles short of our previous day.

We pulled off on the second exit, eventually stopping at a gas station on the left.

"God damn, my ass feels like a blob of lard," I complained.

My phone was frozen, so I couldn't call Bruce. Rhino went inside to ask the gas station attendant if he could use his phone. The guy looked not too keen on us being there. He probably thought we were lunatics for trying to ride bikes in this weather. He did ultimately acquiesce to Rhino's request, but Rhino, clearly drained from the day, wasn't seizing the opportunity. His conversation with Bruce was not going well.

"Dad, listen to me. We are at a gas station in Bemidji. It's the second exit." A few more exchanges ensued. "What are you not getting about this? We are at a gas station. Drive here and pick us up."

It got so bad that Rhino hung up on him, without giving him the proper directions to our location.

"Dude, is he even coming?" I asked.

"Fuck if I know. He doesn't even listen."

"Well, we can't just hope he's coming, bro. Call him back."

"No. He can call me back."

I was furious that Rhino wasn't willing to work with his dad. You only get one dad in life, and here Bruce was doing his best to help his son out, and all Rhino could do was blow up on him. If I spoke to my father the way Rhino was speaking to Bruce, I'd be on the receiving end of a smack across the face. I looked at it like this: the sun was all but set, our day was over, we once again didn't make our mark, and here we were, unable to get the simplest task accomplished. I just wanted to get to the hotel, shower, and unwind.

After some convincing on my part, Rhino got back on the phone. Bruce eventually found us, but then it took another fifteen minutes to load our bikes into the trunk. This delay, coupled with the fact that we didn't want to damage our bicycles during the loading process, only lengthened our time at this desolate gas station in Bemidji.

Bruce pulled out of the gas station, already beginning to debate with Rhino about who was more in the wrong during their phone spat. I couldn't speak. I didn't bother to listen to the barbs they were trading. Physically, I was beginning to get the chills. Mentally, I just wanted some hope that tomorrow would be better, but that felt like asking a lot. The winds of northern Minnesota, during winter's last gasp, were starting to wear on me. It wasn't that I thought continuing on was impossible, but I seriously considered the potential that we would never complete a full day of riding. If the first two days went like this, I had no evidence that tomorrow would be any different.

Soon we got to the Piper Inn in Clearbrook. We checked in, but not before the lady at the desk gave me an earful about how she thought we weren't going to show.

"I almost gave up your room because I thought you guys were going to stand me up."

"Look, lady, it's not like I asked you out on a date," is what I should have said. Instead, "Yeah, we are just running a tad behind. Sorry."

Bruce got settled into his room.

"Where are you going to eat?" he barked at me from the bed of his room.

I remembered that the manager talked about a pizza parlor in town. I looked out the window and noticed that the town could be seen from our hotel. I didn't see a pizza joint, but I figured it couldn't be too hard to find. Bruce didn't explicitly ask for any food, but I could tell from the look in his eye that he would have gladly accepted a pepperoni and sausage.

Rhino and I jumped in Bruce's car and drove a whole sixty seconds to the pizza parlor. There were three kids running the entire operation. I didn't think twice about it. I assumed that's just how things were done on Saturday nights in a small town.

"I'll take Canadian Bacon," I said to one of the kids without any excitement.

Rhino and I sat in the lobby, barely speaking. The Big Buck Hunter video game and claw machine captured my attention and became more important than talking strategy or trying to debate what we could do tomorrow to make our goal attainable.

A man walked up to the counter to pay his bill. He knew one of the kids by name, and the kid was grateful to the man, probably because he gave him a fat tip that he could then spend taking his high school sweetheart to the movies. It made me realize that Clearbrook was no different than St. Cloud, Independence, or Osseo. We are all just people, doing normal things, trying to find happiness in this world.

It was nice to see this man be so generous. I want to be like that when I grow up. I don't need to be wealthy. I only want to have the ability to make a kid's night or spend a hundred dollars on dinner if an old friend comes to visit me. I realize that the older I get, the more money I need. Ironically, as I get older, money has less and less intrinsic value for me. It makes me think about a line I heard in some B-list movie: "Maybe the only thing that we truly could want in life is excess, but instead of money, we would have an excess of time."

Back at the hotel, I thought my body was beginning to betray me. I was beginning to get a cold, and even a steaming hot shower wasn't warming me up. I wrapped myself in as much clothing as possible and picked up the phone as I lied in bed. I called Nicole and my parents to tell them how everything was going.

"I'm cold and I just want the wind to go away," I complained to my dad.

"That's probably not going to happen. You guys signed up for this, so now you gotta deal with it," he said rather plaintively.

"I just hope you're okay," Nicole said when I told her of my physical state. "You're kind of scaring me right now."

There was something disheartening about talking to the outside world while our trip was occurring. It wasn't that I felt disdain for anyone back home. I just thought that this was my time to be away from everyone and everything. It was just Rhino, Bruce, myself, and our bikes whisking us to the border that divided two nations. I didn't want to let people inside my head yet. I wanted everything to process in my brain first. Strategically, I also didn't want people to know we weren't hitting our destinations. It's not so much that I was embarrassed but rather that in people's minds, we were these super humans, two people capable of riding a bicycle four hundred miles in four days. Granted, we were only sixty miles off our pace, but that still wasn't enough for me to want to be on Facebook or reading text messages.

CHAPTER NINE

The next morning, I woke up feeling surprisingly good. The cold I had acquired the previous evening was no longer a deterrent. My legs and lumbar were sore, but nothing ten minutes of warming up couldn't solve. Rhino needed a few extra minutes to get ready, yet he was the one who was calmer. I didn't feel compelled to ask him why he was so calm. With Rhino, I learned it was better not to probe his emotions and just let him be, and trust that his facial expressions were an accurate reflection of how he was feeling.

Once we were ready, we went outside and decided to ride to the Tesoro gas station a few blocks away for breakfast. The attendant was talking to a local man about last night's girls' basketball game. They were dismayed that their girls lost out on a chance to go to the state tournament.

"If Julie would have made that layup, we might be having a different conversation right now," the man said to the woman.

This was one of the little things that reminded me how caught up I was in this trip. I forgot that basketball was my favorite sport. I forgot that I had an intramural championship to win when I got back. I forgot that LeBron James was gearing up for a title run in Cleveland.

Basketball was always what I wanted to do with my life. For years, I dreamed of playing varsity in high school, then getting recruited to play in college for the Ole Miss Rebels. I even dreamed of walking up to the podium on draft night and being selected by the

Minnesota Timberwolves. For the longest time, I was convinced that I would be an NBA basketball player. You always hear NBA players say they knew they were going to make it since they were a young age. Like any kid, I followed that line of thinking. It wasn't until my freshman year of high school did reality start to become apparent.

"If you're good enough, you can play varsity. It doesn't matter that you're a freshman," were the words of an assistant coach, addressing a contingent of young boys just like me.

When I was put on the B team for the freshman, I realized that there was little chance I would play in the NBA. Then my sophomore year I was a role player, limited to playing maybe half the game, if I was lucky. The second to last game of the year, we were playing our rivals, Maple Grove. I made a deep three pointer, then was abruptly pulled from the game. Dismayed, I walked back to the bench, even though it was team policy to always run. I sat down on the bench, not understanding why I was pulled.

Fuck that guy, were the thoughts I had concerning my coach.

"That is the last minute you will ever play for me," said my coach in my face as I fought back tears. "We run off the court at Osseo."

After the game, I changed into street clothes, dejected while the rest of the team celebrated our win. I could have cared less that we won. In that moment, the world was out to get me.

Before I left, my coach pulled me into his office. "Q, I'm going to be honest. You're going to have to work hard to stay on this team."

There is only one game left, I thought to myself.

It was then that I knew I had played my last game for Osseo, and I didn't care. I was so done with playing basketball for them. The only reason I even wanted to be on the team was so that girls would notice me. I didn't actually enjoy playing that year. That was the first year I began to despise the sport, which I attribute to the fact that for the first time in my life, I wasn't the best player on the team.

My chance audible intrusion on the two individual's conversation reminded me that there was a life after my journey. I bought chocolate milk, the same one with the rabbit on the bottle, to go along with a few candy bars and a breakfast sandwich. When I got to the counter, the man took a step back to examine me. The woman behaved no differently, though she was tasked with ringing up my poor nutritional choices. The man cautiously asked where we were headed.

With no hesitation I shot back, "We're biking to Canada, sir."

This statement threw him off, as if I had just told him that all Nicholas Cage films are great.

Rhino followed up behind me. "This is our third day and we are going to be in Winnipeg tomorrow," he said with confidence.

The man and woman looked at each other, frazzled.

"Well, good luck to you guys," the woman said.

The sun had nearly risen when we got back outside. We rode up the first steep hill out of town and got to an overlook that spanned miles. The sun provided a calming relief. When we were driving through a week earlier, we saw a chariot manned by a horse that was extremely peculiar. I suppose to most people, we might have looked not too different on this day.

I decided time and distance were not going to affect me as much as they had the previous two days.

"What do you think about the Milwaukee Bucks?" I asked.

"Sorry?" replied Rhino.

"How do you think they are going to do this year? They just traded for Michael Carter-Williams. He won rookie of the year last year, if I'm not mistaken."

"I don't know. It doesn't even matter because they are going to lose in the first round anyway."

"Dude, you got to get behind your team!"

"I don't even really like basketball," Rhino said, trying to end or divert the conversation topic.

His answers were short, and his tone had a bite. I understood where he was mentally. He was locked in and just wanted to put his head down and ride. Yet I needed him on this day. I needed him to keep my spirits up.

Soon after our dead-end conversation, my back began to seize up. We made it another two miles before I told him I needed to stretch.

"Dude, I just need a minute. My back is hollering at me right now."

We stopped at another little gas station. Rhino went in, and I did my best to get my lumbar fired up and feeling good. My lumbar has always caused me problems. It started when we went to Rice the previous August, right when we had reached the overlook of the Mississippi River. During this timeout, my back began to speak to me in an angry dialect. I got off my bike and began to stretch. It never started to feel fantastic until a few miles back into pace.

This trend continued on our longer rides. North Branch felt the same way after we had dinner. There again, I stopped and stretched my back out, which allowed me to coast to the finish line. Someone more knowledgeable than myself in the medical field could probably explain these occurrences better, but all I knew was that getting off my bike and stretching were the keys to alleviating pain and making these journeys successful and enjoyable.

This is what I hoped would happen when Rhino went inside. Granted, we still had eighty-five miles to go before we were in Karlstad, so simply coasting to the finish line was not likely.

Soon after our stop, my lumbar began loosening up. It wasn't to the point where I was pain free, but I definitely was able to continue riding at a decent pace. The problem was that a decent pace was still a horrible pace. The wind had not lessened overnight, so Rhino and I were still merely trudging along. We came to a swooping right turn in the road, and as soon as we veered off, everything changed.

The wind was now on our back, and we began to exponentially increase our pace. This lasted for only a few miles before we had to make a left to get to Brooks. It wasn't all bad though; good riding instincts made me remember where the wind was blowing, and that if we could get going that direction again, we could begin to truly ride.

With the left hand turn completed, markers told us we were only seven miles away from Brooks. For context, that meant we would then be thirty miles in, and only sixty odd miles away from Karlstad, our last overnight stop in the United States. It was only 11:00 a.m. too, so our goal of getting all ninety-five miles was definitely still attainable.

What happened next will go down as the most grueling seven miles of my life. I initially looked at the stretch as a positive, thinking that if we could just swiftly maneuver our way through, we would have a great chance of eating lunch and then having seven or so hours of daylight to travel the last sixty miles. But that didn't happen. The winds we had been feeling all trip were once again blasting in our face. By blasting, I mean they were so strong it would have been just as effective to get off and walk our bikes. Rhino was having more success than myself. He was a good one hundred yards ahead of me for most of this stretch, which was bad because he couldn't block any of the wind from hitting me. I tried to get as low on my bike as I could, but being taller, it didn't matter. The wind continued to drill me from the chest up. I got off my bike about halfway through to stretch. I could barely see Rhino anymore.

I became enraged. I was battling this wind as best I could but to no avail. I started to realize that this was battling on a whole other level. Anything I previously thought of as battling didn't compare. Cars passed me from both lanes, with every one carrying passengers that gazed at how ludicrous I looked. I reestablished position on my bike and pushed the pedals as hard as I could. Every push with my feet felt like a challenge. I couldn't think of anything other than getting to Brooks. I looked forward, thinking that a city limits sign or a restaurant might appear, but each glance was met with disappointment. The process of this hope turning into emptiness happened at least fifteen times. I told myself not to search for false hope, but it didn't work. These seven miles were breaking my spirits.

I caught up to Rhino as we closed in on Brooks. "Sorry, Rhino. I'm doing my best, but that wind is just *nasty*."

"We just got to keep pushing."

"Still, that wind needs to give up at least a little. I could barely move back there."

Rhino slowed his pace so I could ride off his momentum, but the wind still distributed no mercy. A sign appeared that showed us to be two miles from Brooks. I felt like crying because I knew once I checked my phone a time would appear that would be seriously devastating. There would be no way we would get to Karlstad at this snail-like pace. Then, in graceful fashion, Rhino opened up.

"I think I'm done with school."

"What do you mean?" I asked.

"I just don't think school is for me. That's why I'm not taking classes this semester. I just have no interest in it."

"I don't think there is anything wrong with that at all, man. How many credits do you think you have left anyway?"

"I don't know."

"Well, you've gone for like three years now."

"Yeah, but they haven't all been full time semesters."

"Are you officially into your major?"

"No. There are still classes I need just to get into that major."

I was salivating at the insightful dialogue. "Well, you're proba-bly like a sophomore then."

"That sounds about right."

"I'll be honest, Rhino. I don't love going to school either, but there are a lot of parts about it I enjoy. Sure I'd rather be making money, but there are a lot of positives to school. It's a great place to meet people."

"Well, yeah, but I'm not a big social person."

"Still, you like to party," I said, a large smile on my face.

"Duh."

Brooks came into view and we took a left off the county road to meet Bruce at the gas station. Rhino opening up to me, if only for a short time, meant a lot. He was not big on sharing his feelings, and I always had to probe him for some sort of insight into his life. Yet in that moment, we had an honest, open dialogue. It was these moments that made Rhino special. Like he said, he wasn't the most verbal, but every now and then, he would share a heartfelt sentiment and blow me away with his candidness.

Lost in this journey was what riding meant to the both of us. If not for riding, I don't know if he and I would be friends. It brought us together and was a way for each of us to evolve a hobby into a passion. Most people have friends they've bonded with through special circumstances or trying times, and this situation was no different. We both chose to go through the physical trials, all for the sake of proving that we could do it. Our ambitions ultimately defined our friendship, and that connection was one that couldn't have been found on a whim. It made me realize how lucky I was to have someone like Rhino in my life; someone who wanted to do the impossible and who wanted me to be there with him for it.

In Brooks, I was so apprehensive to look at my phone because I was afraid we had just lost about two hours. My fears were confirmed. It was 1:00 p.m. We walked into the gas station. Bruce was chatting with some older folks who were sitting near him. I saw Bruce holding our newspaper article, and when he saw us, a look of joy spread across his face. The people he was sitting with turned to face us, and they were starstruck that we were in their presence. Two younger people, with snowmobile suits on, were now looking at us. They were also surprised to see us. I suppose if one second I was reading a newspaper article about two people, and then the next moment they were in front of me, I might be starstruck as well.

I went to the bathrooms, impressed at how clean they were. I grabbed some chicken fingers, a side of cheese curds, and a small bag of peanuts, all of which was unreasonably expensive.

This was one of the problems of the trip. We ended up eating mostly in gas stations or at restaurants that were lacking in nutritional value because we were always pressed for time. We couldn't pack healthy snacks because they would freeze in our bags. At times, this was more of an excuse than an actuality. Sure, we could have put food in Bruce's SUV or ate bananas at gas stations, but the last thing I wanted to eat after enduring physical hardship was a banana. I always opted for nachos or donuts, justifying the poor decision by saying I was going to burn the carbs off. Being a slender person whose only defining feature was a somewhat chiseled core, I would burn off the carbs and calories of each unhealthy item I ate, but that doesn't mean those bags of chips were good for my system. I needed to be eating food that would give me energy and allow me to sustain the feeling of being satiated for longer periods of time. Eating crap food only made my life harder. Even as I was mashing down fistfuls of cheese curds, I knew I was doing a disservice to myself, but I simply did not care.

With this knowledge, it was easy to see why people abuse substances and develop bad addictions. It is so much easier to mask pain or unhappiness than to deal with it. I did this when both Stephanie, and later Nicole, cheated on me. I resorted to drinking as a means of coping. It helped for the day, night, or whenever I felt like getting drunk. Still, it didn't solve any of my problems. I'd still wake up the next day hungover, feeling just as shitty about my bad luck as before, only this time I had to deal with physical pain as well as emotional hardship.

There was a time when I felt that getting cheated on was a part of life. After all, it happened to me twice in a six-month span. I began to think that cheating was normal in a relationship. People are unfaithful to each other every day. Instead of merely chalking up my circumstances to bad luck, I began to revolt.

Nicole later left to go back to work at Deep Portage for the summer, and while she was gone, I made it a point to explore my faux freedom. I'd go to the bars every weekend and dance with all sorts of women in ways that if Nicole saw, she would have dumped me in an instant. I approached women and struck up conversations for the thrill of talking to other women. I spent a night at the house of a woman Nicole despised, and I didn't tell her about it until she returned from camp. While I never physically cheated on Nicole, emotionally I was the biggest jerk in St. Cloud.

Nicole would come home some weekends, and we would have an amazing time together. We would go out to eat, watch movies, and lay in bed for hours, having sex and laughing like life was the greatest joy. We even went to the same bars I would be emotionally unfaithful to her. There were never any complications, and because of that, I would go back every weekend she was not around and continue to do my same selfish behavior.

Yet this wasn't because I didn't love Nicole or because I felt that I was in the clear for doing what I did. I no longer cared that Nicole had cheated on me. I loved her and was able to move past her error in judgment. I did what I did because I followed my immature emotions and desires, the same ones that guided me through my first eighteen months living in St. Cloud.

I never thought I was wrong either. To me, as long as I never put my tongue in some woman's mouth or other parts of my body in inappropriate places, I was morally clear. When Nicole returned, I simply stopped, convinced that I had a metaphorical switch I could turn on and off that would control my sexual desires and my love for finding fulfillment from women that gave me attention, if only because they considered me attractive.

This was also part of what made my time in St. Cloud so self-revelatory. Before I moved there, I had only slept with two women. The first was a very nice woman who saw me as boyfriend material. I saw her as someone I could take twenty years of sexual repression and frustration out on. Our relationship ended when I came to the realization that I wasn't dating her for anything other than physical, selfish reasons. In what I considered to be an appropriate decision, I broke up with her because I felt guilty for leading her on.

The very next day, I regretted it, but not because I suddenly realized I had an affinity for her. I regretted it because my balls started to ache, and I feared that it would be too long before I was lucky enough to have sex again. My muscles began to shake. It dawned on me that I would be going from having sex nearly every day to complete abstinence.

"What would you think if I got back together with Mindy?" I remember asking my mom at our kitchen table.

She knew why I broke up with her, and therefore most likely knew why I was thinking about seeking a reunion.

"Don't you ever do that to her," my mom growled at me, her face turning red at even thinking about me doing what I wanted to do.

Eventually I did have one more dalliance with Mindy, in the bathroom of my brother's house, about a week later. I was babysitting my nephew and could no longer disregard my urges. I called her up and asked her to come over, the same place where she had taken my virginity months earlier. I knew she would come over because she still liked me.

"Perhaps we could just take a break for two years while you go to St. Cloud," she offered, her face beaming at the potential of us reuniting at some point.

"Yeah, we could try that I guess."

I felt so low. I didn't actually want to get back together with Mindy. It wasn't anything she did either. She simply was not someone I deemed compatible. All I wanted was to get naked and make myself feel better. I didn't even have the decency to walk her to the door. It was the last time I ever saw Mindy.

In the second of my pre-St. Cloud relationships, I had been involved with the most fascinating woman I have ever met. Her name was Zoe and she helped shape my personal and sexual ideologies. Zoe was roughly five feet and seven inches, her hair a curly, golden blonde that took my breath away when the sun bounced off of it.

The same summer I was to leave for St. Cloud, we met on a dating site. The whole summer, she and I clicked. We did many things together, but not everything. She kept me at bay, most likely strategically, to keep either of us from getting emotionally over-invested. Zoe showed me what a real woman was all about. She was so confident, walking with an aura that captivated me with every step she took. We would sit in my parent's basement, watch artful films, drink Arnold Palmers, and talk about various subjects.

"Did you have a boyfriend at all this last school year?" I probed.

"No, but there was this one guy who turned out to be a total dick."

"What'd he do?" I asked, my curiosity peaked.

"Oh, God," Zoe began. "So essentially this guy lied to me just so I would have sex with him."

"That doesn't sound too surprising," I said, knowing the type of guy she was referencing.

"Well, the thing about it is, I told him all along that we didn't have to date to have sex."

"What do you mean by that?"

Zoe's face grew sterner. "I don't have to be dating someone to want to have sex. This guy though. He kept telling me how he wanted to date me. Finally, one night we had sex. The very next morning he left and later told me that he never actually wanted to date me."

My heart sank listening to Zoe's experience. "I'm so sorry that happened to you."

"It's not a big deal. It's not like I can't find someone else," said Zoe, laughing and her hair flipping to the side, stealing my gaze and sympathy all at the same time.

It was then that I realized Zoe wasn't like any other woman I had ever met. Her confidence made me more confident. Her care-free, liberated take on sex opened my eyes to how life could be, and not in a tasteless way. Zoe gave me the greatest lesson of my life: that women were just as sexual as men, only less frontal about it.

After our talk, Zoe climbed on top of me and we began making out. I ran my fingers through her hair, making sure it wasn't a bother so that I could stare directly into her eyes.

"Do you want to have sex?" I asked, the moment feeling so right.

"I don't know. I barely know you and I don't know enough about your past."

"That's totally cool, Zoe. I get it. I'm not trying to pressure you at all."

A long silence ensued. We stared into each other's eyes, just basking in the moment and feeling fulfilled with our revealing conversation. Zoe leaned down and breathed hot, radiant air into my ear.

"I trust you," she whispered ever so softly.

My heart nearly jumped out of my chest. Zoe took off her shirt and the next couple of minutes made for the most erotic experience of my life.

My poor eating habits were also bad for my wallet. I ended up spending almost ten dollars every time I walked into a gas station. This wasn't devastating, but considering I was eating processed garbage and not natural foods, I was mired in a pathetic cycle. I certainly should have put ten dollars into a nice steak and potatoes, or even some fresh fruit. In fairness, there was something about gas station fruit that screamed "Hell no!" The healthiest thing I consistently consumed was definitely water. Once again, the problem with water is that the more I drank, the more I had to dispose of, which meant more stops and less riding. It wasn't easy to simply hold off on urinating. The cold forced the need for more stops, the equivalent to drinking ice water as opposed to tap water. Still, the worst part about having to go was exposing myself on the side of the road to oncoming traffic in frigid conditions. Now not only was my midsection subzero, many northern Minnesota residents now knew I was not well endowed.

After paying for my food and then sitting down next to Bruce, I once again felt inclined to punch him in the face. He immediately began lamenting the fact that it was 1:00 p.m., and we had only traveled forty miles. I thought about telling him that it was the last nine miles that took us two hours, but I didn't think he would have understood the injustice nature had levied upon us.

In that moment, a feeling then came over me. I had genuinely forgot what day of the week it was. I wasn't under the constraints of a schedule, so to speak. I was just living in the world. The day of the week didn't matter. The only semblance of placement I had was the sun. It was one of the first times I felt truly autonomous from society, like nothing else really mattered.

"We're still going to make it to Karlstad," Rhino told Bruce.

Bruce chuckled. "Yeah. You guys will get there at midnight."

I believed Rhino. The morning was turning to afternoon, and all we needed was one break in the wind, and we would be right back on schedule.

That break came instantaneously. We left the gas station and merged onto the highway. This highway was literally the last road we would be on in the United States. We still had well over one hundred miles before we would be in Winnipeg, but we were only sixty miles away from Karlstad. If we rode until sundown, that would mean we'd need to average only ten miles per hour the rest of the day. That estimate also didn't account for riding after sunset, when we would still be able to ride in limited light. It was comparable to our first trip to Brainerd, when we left at 3:00 p.m. but still made it before 10:00 p.m.

The wind that breezed us forward a few hours ago when we made our first right turn was now on our backs, and it would be on our backs until we got to Thief River Falls. We also had the added benefit of cars going sixty to seventy miles per hour past us, which would give us even more of a boost. Adding to that, we were now on a highway that would be heavily labeled with distance markers.

After a period of what felt like no time at all, I looked up and we were already ten miles in. We were now doing our best riding of the trip. We were back to the same proficiency we had exhibited in the fall. The first stretch out of Brooks felt like the last leg when we came back from Alexandria. We had all the momentum, and the rest of the day looked positive.

Time continued to pass, but we continued to blaze the highway. We were only six miles away from Thief River Falls and the sun was at its highest point. A casino was coming up on the left, and I noticed many cars turning that direction. I figured when we passed that turn, things would clear up, but they did not. We were now being squeezed because our shoulder was narrowing and we were going to have to ride on the actual highway with the speeding cars.

The shoulder soon completely vanished, but we were in Thief River Falls. This meant we only had thirty miles to go. Thief River Falls was one of those weird towns. It's only a short distance from Canada, and very far from the metro, but it's quite large. They had a Target and a few hotels.

We veered off to stop at a Holiday gas station. It was our last planned stop before Karlstad. We took our turns using the bathroom. I bought some cheese crackers to fuel me the last thirty miles. I estimated we had two hours left before the sun would set. This put us on the brink of getting to Karlstad before sunset if we could keep our fifteen-mile per hour pace.

We navigated through the remainder of Thief River Falls. The town's latter half was beautiful, even for gloomy March. We were on a sidewalk the whole time. We passed a park where grass was beginning to faintly show. We came to our last right turn, the one that would have us continue on the same highway headed for the border. This turn signaled the end of our run with that harrowing wind on our backs, but we were guaranteed it wouldn't be in our faces.

Five miles after the turn, the wind wasn't killing us. It was no longer helping us, but it wasn't crippling our plans like it did earlier in the day. The day was beginning to turn to night. There were roughly twenty miles to go before Karlstad when we hit another snag. Rhino was beginning to push ahead of me as I could feel my back continue to tighten.

"I need a stretch," I yelled.

"We got to keep going. Give it a few more miles, brother. There is a gas station coming up soon."

I didn't think I could do it. The pain felt irreversible. I began to get frustrated because we were so close to Karlstad, and we didn't have a lot of daylight left to work with. Rhino was now out of sight, and I kept forcing myself to push. I should have stopped and loosened my back up, but my ibuprofen was in Rhino's bag. I thought stretching would only be a temporary fix. I needed some medicine.

I could feel my legs no longer wanting to turn. We were in the eighty-mile range for the day, and I could feel everything giving out. The muscles above my knees sent a sharp discomfort to my brain with every revolution of the pedals. Finally, it became too much. I stopped on the side of the road. I put my kickstand down and began moving as much of my body as I could. There was no blood flow in my lower half. I could not lift each leg up comfortably. I wiggled my butt around, hoping that would provide relief for my back. Cars passed me, and I hoped none of them would stop. I looked up at the sky. It was a beautiful combination of yellow and red, and all I could do was just look at it for a few minutes.

When I came out of my daze, I knew I had to catch up to Rhino. I slowly eased back into a pace. A few more minutes passed before I heard Rhino calling my name.

"Q! Q! Q!"

I thought an animal was mauling him. His voice came from the left and I saw that he had pulled off and was waiting for me in a park.

By the time I saw him, I was past the road to the park so I halfheartedly looked over my shoulder and made a wild left turn, narrowly
missing bumping into a car that was in my blind spot.

When I got off my bike and looked into my bag, I was down to
four cheese crackers, meaning we had to get to Karlstad sooner than
later. Just like his father, Rhino began chirping me about my speed.

"You absolutely can't go that slow. We need to keep going
because it is going to be pitch black soon."

"Dude, my back is killing me and you have the pills. I could
barely stand at one point." I was conflicted as to whether I should tell
Rhino to fuck off or just focus on getting the ibuprofen in my system
and flowing through my veins. "All right, listen. You can't leave me
hanging like that. You don't have a phone and what if my bike broke
down? Then we'd be fucked."

"Well, we're too close to just stop," Rhino said.

"Dude, I'm not trying to stop. I want to finish this day as bad as
you. We just need to communicate and be more responsible."

I swallowed three pills of ibuprofen and danced around to get
my blood flowing. I knew it would take some time for the pills to
take effect. Painfully, I got back on my bike and we eased into riding.
After a few miles, I felt much better. I knew my muscles just needed
an extended break, especially considering we had never rode this far
nor done three consecutive days before. I didn't feel tired though.
Through everything, I knew I still had energy in my body to get this
day done. It was all about keeping certain muscles relaxed and my
mind sharp.

Within an hour the sun was gone, we had lost our pace, and
we were officially in the black. Yet there were only eight miles to go.
Rhino and I stopped to stretch and mentally prepare for the unknown
we were about to ride through. We needed this to complete our first
full day of riding, where we make our goal and settle for nothing less.

Rhino took the middle of the road and I closer to the shoulder.
Our synchronicity and collectivity would be what would get us to
Karlstad. As we began, it became clear that the roads were not well
maintained. There were cracks near the median, in the middle of the
right lane, and on the shoulders. There was no consistency in terms

of a safe pathway. Our lights shone ahead for about ten feet. After ten feet, we were running a risk.

The wind died down and we started to make headway. Along with that, we now were cutting our reaction times short, meaning the faster we went, the less likely one of us would be able to see a pothole that could potentially end our trip.

We were parallel to a railroad track, which was somewhat comforting, but what remained beyond that were miles of woods, which I assumed contained wolves, foxes, moose, and other animals that might see our blinking lights and wonder if it was a food source. We were both scared out of our minds.

"Just keep pushing," said Rhino. "We *will* get there."

We passed a restaurant that was filled with cars. A few streetlights helped guide us for a couple hundred feet after the restaurant. After that, there was literally no light coming from anything other than our bikes and the stars.

My film palette must have included too many horror movies because every time I heard a cricket chirp, I thought we were going to be attacked. I kept thinking I was going to have to become Liam Neeson in *The Grey*, surviving against a pack of massive, bloodthirsty wolves.

"There is nothing out there. The faster we ride, the better we will be," I kept repeating.

The only noise besides our bikes was the continued chirping of millions of crickets. Their noise provided a calming relief, although it didn't mean anything if a wolf blindsided either one of us. I could hear sticks breaking along the railroad. I became convinced that something was following us, waiting only for the perfect time to attack.

"If it bites me, run it over," I said to Rhino.

I figured I would take the brunt of any attack because I was on the inside of the road. The sticks started breaking less and less. I thought I was going to piss my pants. Either this thing was losing pace or it was about to make its move.

We passed a sign that noted Karlstad was two miles away. I could see the lights of what was presumably the city. They were the first lights we had seen since the restaurant. Two more miles were all we needed to knock out our first complete day and to reach safety.

As we neared, I gradually became more convinced we had out-run whatever was following us. I figured there was another mile to go when I heard another stick break.

"Keep going!" I yelled.

A car was now on our rear. For the first time during our whole trip, I was relieved to see a car because I wanted its lights to scare off whatever was lurking. As the car neared, the tall grass on my right became more and more visible.

"*Scare it off. Scare it off,*" I continually whispered and pleaded to myself.

In my fear, I had neglected to notice how well my legs were pumping. The adrenaline negated any soreness I had. As the car passed, I kept pedaling as hard as I could. I wasn't convinced we were safe until we hit the main stretch of Karlstad.

We made it, passing through the downtown that looked eerily similar to the one in Brainerd. It was an easing feeling because now the only things on my right were houses. We had arrived, but this time it was purely business.

We were too late for the hotel owner's comfort. She simply left the keys to our room on the office door. Our room had only two beds, a TV, and a shower, but it was all we needed. We put our bikes away and Rhino went to Bruce's room to grab his car keys and tell him we made it.

We once again drove to a nearby gas station. Everything was overpriced, per usual. For ten dollars I obtained two sandwiches, some crackers, and chocolate milk. It's not exactly what a college student would call bargain hunting.

"It's a five-dollar minimum on cards," a middle-aged man with a gray beard snarled at me when I placed my food on the counter.

"No worries, sir. I got you," I replied.

The man gave me a perturbed look as I grabbed my food and walked to the car. When I got back in, I couldn't find the room key, and we only had one. I frantically looked all over, feeling every part of my body in desperate search for that stupid key. Rhino got back in and I had to continue looking in a way that wouldn't make Rhino think I had actually lost it.

We got back to the hotel, and I had to finally admit that I couldn't find it.

"Dude, I might be losing my mind here, but do you have the key? I can't find it." Rhino's face turned even redder than what the freezing March air had already done to his complexion. "I mean, I have it, but I don't know where it is. I swear I just put it in my coat pocket."

Rhino was irate, and I don't blame him. How could I lose a room key in a matter of minutes?

I looked all over the car, through my pockets, even in my sandwich, but it was nowhere to be found. I started looking under cars, purely out of frantic desperation.

"I'm going up to my dad's room. Text me when you find it," Rhino said after a few minutes of rolling his eyes and waiting.

Alienated, I sat on the curb and finished my sandwich. Two men from another room walked past, most likely mistaking me for the first homeless man in Karlstad's history. I dialed the number of the woman who left the keys. Fortunately she answered and let us in, all the while I tried to explain how weird it was that I couldn't find the key.

All the joy I had gotten out of riding nearly one hundred miles and finally completing a full day just didn't matter anymore. I got inside and went for a shower. Rhino later joined me and we took in the pleasant night. We watched an NFL free agency show on ESPN and ate our food, quite content to sit in silence. This was the first night where for me it was hard to get comfortable while lying in bed. My only hope for tomorrow was that lady luck would again favor my physiognomy, and that Canada would welcome us with open arms and little wind.

CHAPTER TEN

Monday, March 9, 2015: the biggest day of them all. This was the day when all our hard work and preparation would come to fruition. The plan was for us to wake up an hour later than usual so we could get the extra rest we missed out on because of the key fiasco. Then we would travel the last thirty miles of US territory before making our way into Canada. At that point, we would only have around seventy miles remaining until we were in Winnipeg.

Meanwhile, my dad was driving up from the cities that day to meet us at the border. It wasn't clearly communicated what would happen before or after that. I didn't know if we would beat him to the border or if he would catch up with us after that. This lack of communication would manifest itself in a negative way.

"We'll see you in a few days, Bruce," was the collective sentiment between Rhino and I.

Bruce was set to go to Roseau to check out the high school hockey scene while we had an epic time in Winnipeg. Like the first day, I had to carry the trailer because it had all the stuff we would need that Bruce could no longer transport for us. We lost some time trying to fasten the trailer back onto my bike. It was another reminder of how inept I was at mechanical tasks.

For twenty minutes, I fiddled with the apparatus, trying to connect the heavy trailer to the back of my bike. I finally got it to somewhat stay, and that was good enough for me. I wanted to start riding, and if the trailer fell off, then we would deal with it then.

For breakfast, we scampered across the parking lot to the adjacent grocery store. My blood still boils at how much food cost at this place. Three dollars and fifty cents was the price for a little bottle of chocolate milk. I know I'm not an economics major, but I somewhat understand the costs associated with packaging and distributing food to such a desolate area. So after spending nearly eleven dollars on breakfast, it was time to begin our last thirty miles toward Canada.

The morning was brilliant. Yes, it was windy, but there were many sights to behold. As we left Karlstad, I looked back, knowing this was the last city in Minnesota. The roads were unsurprisingly rocky, as if civilization were trying to warn us what awaited. I spent most of the first couple of miles dodging potholes and scanning up ahead in hopes that this minefield of a road would soon clear up.

We passed what appeared to be an abandoned trucking stop. My best guess was that this used to be the last checkpoint in America before truckers had to venture all the way into Canada. Our pace was decent. My knees were beginning to feel like a ball of rubber bands. Every lift of each knee yielded a different result. Sometimes I felt agony at the ball that was stuck on the top of my knee. Other times, I felt that this was all worth it. I was going to get off my bike at some point that day and feel like royalty. Suddenly I got a call from my dad.

"Good morning. Where are you guys?"

"We are about fifteen miles from the border, dad. How about you?"

"Well, I left early this morning and I'm probably about only twenty minutes behind you guys."

Twenty minutes behind us? I told him not to leave until later in the day, but my dad is the restless type that can't sit still for more than five minutes, unless he just gets home from work and sits down in front of the TV; at that point, he is practically immovable for the remainder of the evening.

"Dad, we still have a lot of riding left. You are way too early."

"I know but let's just talk about it when we meet up."

"Um, I know there is a gas station coming up. I think it's a Cenex. We can pull off and meet you there if you want."

A few seconds of pause ensued. I didn't know if it was a bad phone connection or contemplation on my dad's part.

"That sounds good, Quent. I'll see you there."

I hung up my phone feeling irritated. He was not supposed to be here that early in the day, and now our plans might have to be readjusted.

"What was that all about?" Rhino inquired.

"My dad says he is only about twenty minutes behind us."

"What the fuck? He's way early. We aren't even to the border yet."

"I know. I don't know what to say. We are going to meet him at the gas station up ahead."

We arrived at the gas station, a sense of uneasiness pervading the mood. Don't get me wrong, my dad is a great guy. Still, he has his way of doing things. When I first saw his 2006 Honda Odyssey pull up, I was happy. I thought, okay, this is the furthest away from home I have ever seen my dad, save for our family vacation to Florida in the eleventh grade. He had a weird look on his face. I couldn't tell if he was happy that I was alive or shocked that we had made it this far. As mentioned, he is a bicycle enthusiast as well, so at some point I expected some envy to become visible.

"You guys are almost there," he began, breaking the ice.

My uncle Chuck was supposed to be with him. "Where is Uncle Chuck?" I asked.

"Something came up."

This was a disappointing reality because I always admired how well Rhino and my uncle Chuck got along. The first night they met, at my cabin, they stayed up all hours of the night drinking Grey Goose Redbulls. There was a mutual respect there that I would have liked to see in action once again.

"Oh, Quent," said my dad, looking at my patchwork job attaching the trailer. "Don't you remember that I showed you how to put this trailer on before you left? You have it hanging by a thread."

"I know but that thing is messed up. I tried for twenty minutes to get it on and it just wouldn't go."

"Well, it took me about five seconds to clip it on," said my father in a sarcastic, patronizing tone.

"Good for you," I retorted.

"You guys only have seven more miles to go until the border."

This fact made me happy. As I looked out, all I could see were muddy tire tracks and a small park with a swing set. A few people came in and out of the gas station, but none of them paid any attention to us.

Just like that, an unceremonious reunion between my father and I. As always, things were awkward when we were about to depart.

"I guess we'll see you at the border then, Dad."

This was about the time when Rhino and I turned from exhausted adventurers to giddy teenage school boys who had just found a box of Playboys underneath our older brother's bed. We were seven miles away. In other words, we were *this* close to breathing Canadian air. Those last seven miles were a whirlwind of emotions.

As we rode, everything just felt right. The sun was shining. Rhino and I were flying. Four cars passed us, making the appreciated effort to veer all the way into the left lane to avoid clipping us. One of them honked, presumably in support. My emotions were all over the place. I had never been so excited. The wind seemed to die down for the next half hour, so we could enjoy the moment. I looked to my left and noticed a tiny house that had a mailbox at the beginning of the driveway. This person had found peace, and it was this far north. I had told Dave DeLand at the *Times* that I was worried about bears and wolves, but those fears were not a part of my current thought process. It was just Mother Nature, two ergonomically sufficient machines, plus Rhino and I.

We stopped at the border sign.

"Take a picture of me next to this," Rhino asked.

It felt like an iconic moment. I framed Rhino standing next to the sign, his finger pointing at the Canada label. Before I snapped the photo, I looked at him, wanting to take in the moment with my own eyes before the flash inside my phone went off.

Rhino and I didn't concoct the cure for cancer or raise the flag at Okinawa, but we did something unprecedented. We had grinded through northern Minnesota in the dead of winter on our bicycles. We didn't have any fancy equipment or sponsors. We had each other, and that propelled us to where we were. I thought of our first trip to Brainerd, how accomplished I felt then. This moment was ten times more gratifying.

"That's a hell of a start, bro," I said when I returned to Rhino, knowing we were only halfway done with our journey.

"Yes. A great start indeed," said Rhino, his head facing the ground, but still his smile more than obvious.

I haven't heard a lot of criticism from pundits regarding our trip, other than the occasional verbal jab from a friend or relative. I was always curious what one of them might say to one of us. It's sad that people always attempt to diminish other's accomplishments. In fairness, I do the same, and am probably the most sardonic individual in my close circle. Yet for whoever is laying it all on the line, these critics become the biggest motivation. In this instance, if it wasn't for my dad or friends telling me we couldn't do it, where would we have gotten the inspiration? When my knees were buckling and my legs screamed for a break, it was their negativity that pushed me to persevere.

At that moment I had forgotten all the bad things that happened to me in my time in St. Cloud. I forgot about having developed mono, rendering me incapable of having fun for three weeks. I forgot about having to go to the doctor to get an STD check, twice. Even though all the tests had come back negative, I still felt contaminated for my wild behavior. I forgot about Scooter and me brawling at a party one night after he drank too much, putting our friendship at stake. I forgot about for a whole semester I was forced to sit next to a woman Mason and I had catfished, punishment for my immature and degrading behavior.

Lastly, I let go of my pain and sadness from being cheated on. It didn't matter anymore. I had proved to myself that getting to Canada showed I could do anything. I didn't need any of that negativity in my life, no matter how self-inflicted it was. Sometimes in life you just have to let go and enjoy what you have in front of you, no matter how little it may seem.

When we rolled into the border, it went much smoother than the first time. The patrols were expecting us, so once we showed them our passports, we were free to go. A large woman who had french fry stains on her breast pocket congratulated us.

"Great job, you two. Have fun in Winnipeg."

"Well, what do you guys want to do?" my dad started when we reconvened with him in Canadian territory.

"I want to take a photo next to the Welcome to Canada sign. That's all I want to do right now," I said.

I went in front of the sign and flipped the camera on my phone around to face me. Snap, snap, snap. I'm sure I got one good one during that barrage.

"You looked so sexy in that photo," Nicole would later say to me.

"What do you want to do, Rhino?" I asked, turning his direction. He shrugged. We felt like we had made it. I was ready to throw down and celebrate right there.

"Why don't you guys ride a few miles ahead and I'll pick you up there?" my dad suggested.

Rhino and I silently deliberated and then agreed to stop riding up ahead. Neither of us wanted to be the one to cut short our day, but we both wanted off our respective bikes.

We rode five more miles just to say we had ridden our bikes in Canada, with the wind completely at our backs. Within minutes, we had already arrived at the spot where we would meet my dad. They were celebratory miles, a reminder of all we had accomplished.

We placed our bikes on my dad's hitch and headed for Winnipeg. It was a surreal feeling sitting in the van, a vehicle I had traveled in so often growing up. This time the van traveled to me.

"You should be proud of yourselves," my dad said. "Not many people will ever do what you two just did."

Coming from his cynical mouth, his sentiments meant so much. My dad was initially baffled at our idea, but as it became a reality, to hear him say that meant he believed in me.

"Sometimes the most stupid ideas are the most successful," he would always say.

To pass the time, I read a story in the *Star Tribune* on Gary Neal, a newly acquired player for the Timberwolves, and how he would like to stick around Minnesota after the season ends. It was another indicator of my past, how I spent so many days and nights with my family going to the cabin, reading the sports section of the newspaper on the way there.

I vividly recall the summer of 2006, when the Minnesota Twins burst onto the MLB scene. That year, Joe Mauer won his first batting title and Justin Morneau won the American League MVP. The Twins would eventually win the division title on the last day of the season. That season was when I fell in love with the Twins, avidly following their progress in the newspaper every day.

Being a passenger as we made our way across the vast terrain was different from the week before, when I was driving. Everything became more real and tangible. The trees looked more inviting, like they needed to see we would return before they unearthed their beauty. The poorly maintained roads became a symbol of something else, of a journey not yet completed.

I soon reminded myself we were only halfway done. We had completed the new, fun part of the journey; the part that everyone cared about. The way back through familiarity would cement Rhino and I in biking lore.

CHAPTER ELEVEN

In the last couple of years, I didn't need many reasons to celebrate. Celebrating was an excuse to be immature. Celebrating provided me an outlet I had never fully explored. This time, in Winnipeg, there was a reason to celebrate. Winnipeg wasn't much different from any major American city. They have all the fast food spots a junkie could want. Museums and art engulf their downtown business district. Hockey was the main attraction in Canada, and that was evident as banners lined the streets, full of various players and their accompanying insignia splayed for all who pass to see.

Rhino and I were in the city, ready to party, but we had nowhere to stay. With no mobile Internet because of T-Mobile's excruciatingly high international fees, it was decided that we had to get to a spot that had Wi-Fi. Tim Horton's was that place. After about twenty unnecessary minutes spent in the Canadian conglomerate trying to simply connect to the Internet, we finally made some progress on a place to stay.

"Why is everyone staring at us?" I asked Rhino.

"Dude, you have got to get over yourself. You're not that good looking."

"But seriously, I think everyone is looking at us. Should I go buy something so we don't seem like mooches?"

"I thought your dad said we could go to Subway."

"I suppose, but this is weird."

"Just shut the fuck up. I just booked us one."

"Where at?"

"Days Inn. It's not too far from here."

"Okay, well let's get back out there. My dad probably thinks we are eating here."

We walked back out and told my dad of our reservation.

Then, my dad embarrassed me. "It's cool if I stay in your guys' room, right? Rhino, do you care? Quent and I can share a bed."

"I don't mind at all," Rhino said, underneath a sheepish grin that soon turned into a chuckle.

I didn't want to have to share a bed with my dad. He always slept in only his underwear and his whole body always was covered in massive amounts of hair.

"Keep fucking laughing, Rhino. Hopefully Bruce doesn't need a room on the way back." I growled.

We hadn't been on our bikes for about two hours, but time seemed to last forever. The hotel we were at read about our journey in the *Winnipeg Sun* and gave us a free compartment to store our bikes for the next few days, which was stellar, considering normally we had to make space for them in our rooms.

We got up to the room, and on cue, I prepared for our phone interview with MPR.

"You guys will be on the air tomorrow. If the hotel tries to charge you for this call, tell me, and we will pay for the bill. We really just want this interview," said Kryssy Pease from MPR.

Neither Rhino nor myself had ever been on the radio before, so for us this was a thrilling moment.

"Kryssy, this is for sure going to be on the air, right?" I asked.

There was a sense of uneasiness stemming from my first encounter with her. It was before we had left that she had interviewed us, but she never aired our chat. I held some resentment from this because I felt our story was a noteworthy ordeal. In all honesty, it probably wasn't her decision whether our segment aired. Still, the reality that we had made it probably was what pushed us onto the radio and also what probably kept us off initially. I understood. Radio executives don't want to run a segment on a couple college kids who may or may not live up to their lofty expectations.

"This is definitely going to be on the air. What happened last time was simply unfortunate. I'm sorry for that, Q."

"It's not the end of the world. I would just like to know we are going to be on the air."

"I totally understand. How about when you and I are done, you hand the phone over to Rhino?"

"That sounds good," I said as I swiveled in a black leather chair next to a desk.

"Okay, so where to begin . . . All right, so how was the journey?"

I inhaled, planning to unleash a blizzard of quotes. "To start, Kryssy, it was crazy. Just an eclectic mix of emotions."

Eclectic. I first heard the word in a psychology class when my spastic professor was describing personality disorders. "Many people have eclectic personalities," she would say. I don't know what made me think to use that word, but at the time it seemed so right.

"What was the most difficult part of the trip?" Kryssy then asked.

I told her about the previous day when we had to battle through horrible winds just to get to Brooks. I later made some lame joke that was on par with the title of her radio show, All Things Considered. Secretly, this made me think that I was pretty clever, but the joke never made it on the air. This was highly indicative of why I never went into standup comedy.

After another minute, I handed the phone over to Rhino.

"You talk so fancy," said my dad in a chiding manner.

I needed a moment to be alone and collect my thoughts. I couldn't help but think about the last year and a half, and how much of a struggle it was at times. I found some things out that I previously was oblivious to, like the time Scooter interrupted me when I went to the fridge to grab a peach. "Dude, for the last time, that is a nectarine."

Or how much better sex was without a condom, even though my dad for years told me it felt the same. There was the time when I lied in my room and cried for hours while listening to the saddest music I could find on YouTube, trying to comprehend how someone could cheat on me. "What did I do to deserve this?" was the circuitous thought my brain kept coming to.

I also did some things that, looking back, I regret. I regret trying to go to work at 3:00 a.m. on no sleep, thinking a Redbull would keep me sane. I regret sleeping with my best friend's to-be girlfriend because I was so concerned with trying to prove my masculinity, ultimately costing me a friendship that never recovered from my selfish personality.

I regret the first time I had sex without a condom, with Stephanie, because I thought she loved me, but who in actuality just wanted something new. During our unprotected encounter, I became attached, unable to let go of the love I mistakenly thought I had for her.

It all came full circle two weeks later when she called me, in tears, and told me she had a miscarriage. "I would love to raise a baby girl with you," I told her, half meaning what I said and half scared of what having a child would mean for my future.

But through all this, I lived. I lived life going after something out of the ordinary. Going to Rice, Brainerd, North Branch, and Alexandria made me feel alive. No matter how far away from home or from St. Cloud I was, I always felt alive. The opportunity to be in so much physical distress while at the same time feeling so emotionally euphoric gave me a better buzz than any glass of Grey Goose could ever do for me.

With our arrival in Winnipeg, it also signaled the beginning of another path. By just getting to Winnipeg, I came to the realization that I have the potential to do whatever I wanted to in life. The press and the attention that came with our journey north was great, but the actuality of being in the moment and going through an adventure so demanding was the greatest accomplishment of the first half.

Our first night in Winnipeg, we didn't celebrate as much as I had hoped. On every bike trip, we always talk about how inebriated we are going to get once we settle in. In reality, what always happens is we get to our destination, at which point we're so mentally and physically exhausted that we just want to have a strong beverage and go to bed.

This happened on our first night when we ate at the hotel restaurant.

"These drinks are kind of shitty," Rhino complained. "I've had three and I'm not buzzed."

"Tomorrow we can go to a liquor store," said my dad, trying to be encouraging.

When I went back to the room, I locked myself in the bathroom and Facetimed with Nicole. She was so elated to see me. Her fabulous blonde hair shimmered in what little light there was in her room.

"I'm so proud of you," she said.

There was an awkward pause. I knew she wanted to tell me she loved me but was too bashful to actually say it. I knew I loved Nicole when one night she was blackout drunk at 3:00 a.m. in a bar we weren't legally supposed to be in anymore.

"I have to throw up," she said, stumbling to the bathroom.

I went in with her, knowing full well that the onlookers who were giving me dirty looks thought we had went in to have sex. I held her hair back as she puked up all the rail whiskey and tequila she had been drinking that night.

Nicole loves to drink. It's part of what makes her so attractive. She doesn't drink vodka lemonades or cider beer either, like many sorority girls. She drinks whiskey and IPAs. The drinking dynamic between us was always so unique because I drank like she stereotypically would, choosing Grey Goose sodas to avoid the calories while she chose the high calorie beers and hard liquors.

Nicole was halfway through another round of vomiting when she lifted her head out of the toilet bowl and said to me, "I hate you." Taken aback, I had no idea what to say. "I hate you," she said again.

"Why do you hate me?" I asked, frightened.

I thought this was the truth coming out. I thought maybe someone told her something about me I was trying to conceal. Nicole's head bobbed back and forth. Her body couldn't decide if she was going to throw up again or berate me further.

"I don't care if you hate me," I said. "Because I love you."

Tears began pouring down Nicole's face. I knew then she meant to say love instead of hate.

The next morning, when she woke up, hung over and unsure of what happened the previous night, I told her without revealing the part about me telling her I loved her. She again began crying but in a good way.

I never again told Nicole I loved her until later that summer in the parking lot of a restaurant. I had a lot of drinks and shouldn't have been driving. When I casually glanced her direction, saying it felt so right.

"I love you," I remarked, and we embraced in a passionate kiss.

I never revealed to Nicole that I loved her until then because I was afraid of what that would mean. I knew I loved her, but secretly I wanted her to think that I did not yet. It was another reminder of how selfish and immature I was.

On this night, Nicole was only four hundred miles away, but seeing her on a screen reminded me of how far she and I had come, and how far we still had to go.

The media always depict women as somehow inferior to men, but in most healthy relationships I have seen, there is always an equalitarian dynamic to the partnership. I had that with Nicole. It is a truly a shame that our society has become so riddled with media influence because when we ignore the television screen and immerse ourselves in reality, we start to see how each gender can be a boon to the other.

Nicole taught me a lot about how to care for someone other than myself. I taught her many things relating to the pride and grat-ification she should feel toward herself.

"You're not my property. You're my girlfriend and this is an equal partnership. You are not inferior to me," I'd always tell her.

I wanted her to know that she wasn't just my girlfriend but her own person who was going to be successful in her lifetime on account of her vivacious personality and deep intellect that surfaced whenever she was following her passion, which was teaching.

I hoped our journey to Winnipeg taught someone to follow his or her dreams. Now and then, as I mature and think about myself just a millimeter less, I hope our trip inspired someone to achieve his or her unthinkable. To me, if nothing more ever comes from this journey, I hope that when a child one day achieves his or her dream of becoming a lawyer, professional athlete, etc., they can rightfully say that I had an impact on them. I don't want credit for their accomplishments. I just want someone to say, "That guy made me want to chase my dreams."

CHAPTER TWELVE

The next day we made our way around the city. Winnipeg was the worst when it came to construction, so navigating the city was made even more challenging. I will admit, I am usually one to complain, but when the best place we made it to for a drink was a rundown sports bar, I started to believe that Winnipeg was not as much of an ideal destination as I initially believed.

At the bar, I was reminded of why one should never go to a bar during the middle of the day. The place had a casino-like feel, with gambling machines lining the exterior of the bar and old men occupying the actual bar. Rhino, my father, and I sat at a quiet table located on the perimeter. I ordered a Grey Goose and Redbull. Rhino stuck to beer, and my dad opted for his usual Crown whiskey and water.

Everywhere we went in Winnipeg, the drinks were poorly made. Each place would put exactly one shot of alcohol in a drink. This is commonplace at many places in the United States. Yet in Winnipeg, it is much less subtle. Here, the bartenders pour the alcohol into a shot glass, which then finds its way into the main glass. Ultimately, I wound up with a drink that was one part Grey Goose, eight parts Redbull. I was better off just saving my money and drinking soda.

"God damn, these drinks fucking blow," I cracked, hoping for a buzz that I knew would never come.

"Quent, stop swearing," my dad quickly scolded. "There are other people in here."

"Hopefully they're drunker than I am."

"Why don't you just drink beer?" Rhino asked.

"Bro, you know how much I hate beer."

"Well, what about that time you bought a case of Keystone Light?"

I became pissed off. "Rhino, that was like two months ago. Why are you even talking about that?"

"You think you're so fancy because you drink Grey Goose, don't you?" said Rhino, trying to conjure up an argument.

"And you think you're cool because you're a Packers fan. Give me a break. No one likes people from Wisconsin," I hollered, unable to control myself.

"Quent, that's enough," interjected my dad.

"You're just mad because the Vikings *suck*," Rhino said, having successfully pissed me off.

"Ryan, the Packers for a long time weren't that good either. I think it was in the '60s they had many bad years," my dad politely informed us. "Sports are so ebb and flow."

"See, motherfucker. Talk to me now about how good the Packers are," seizing my chance to be a dick.

Rhino angrily placed his drink on the table and glared at me. For five seconds, I felt like smashing his face in. I assumed he felt the same. We both looked prepared to fight, but then once the initial anger subsided, we both realized neither of us actually knew how to fight.

Soon we left and made our way around the city some more, stopping at a liquor store and Target. The liquor store was gigantic. They had everything under the sun, including my beloved Grey Goose. The issue was that because of Canada's heavy sales tax, a bottle of Grey Goose that would normally be $55 was instead priced at $100. Sadly, I had to defer to the much more reasonable Smirnoff. Rhino bought a case of citrus beer.

At Target, everything was a mess. All the Targets in Canada were closing down because they were not performing well. When we went in, it was evident why. I had wanted to buy a pair of jeans because I forgot to pack pants for going out. I found the most elegant pair there, which wasn't saying much, and headed for a changing room. Once there, I had to navigate heaps of clothing just thrown on the ground.

"Sorry. We don't clean them out anymore," said a chunky man with odd looking glasses.

Out of fear more than necessity, I bought the pair of jeans that were similar to what I would wear in high school. I felt like a young boy again, going to Target with my mom to look for new clothes while everyone else went to Hollister or American Eagle.

"Oh, those look really nice on you," my mom would usually say when I would walk out of the changing room with a look of disgust on my face. I could never tell if she was fashionless or ignorant to my disposition. Sadly, this sort of shopping stretched into my high school years, a time when I was more likely to win the lottery than land a date to the prom.

We then went back to the hotel and grabbed our dirty laundry from the first leg of the adventure and headed to a Laundromat. I changed out of dirty sweatpants and into my new poorly faded jeans. Since in Canada the currency was so different, we had to exchange ours for theirs at the washing venue. Fortunately the woman there recognized that we were tourists and was extremely accommodating.

We were only doing laundry, but that woman taught me something. So often in America we look down upon people who are unfamiliar with our way of doing things. We become impatient and do not want to take the extra time to teach others. I am not absolved of guilt. I too am impatient with others, and not just people from out of state, or from a different nation. I become impatient if the road ahead is fifteen miles long and I want to be there that instant. I become impatient if the person driving in front of me is only five miles over the speed limit. Impatience, to me, is the compounding of too many little things that I let bother me. Instead of becoming upset about what I don't have, it is many times appropriate to relax and acknowledge what I do have. This binary way of thinking is not newfound, but when actually implemented in one's life, becomes a precursor to happiness.

Taking this thought a step further, the most gratifying things in life occur when I slow down and embrace the moment. When I stop thinking so much about the next thing or the better thing, I then can begin to see the sheer humanism in other people, and how essential it is that I prioritize others so that I can improve the world in which I live. This is partly why I was able to date Nicole, because I stopped thinking about the next hook up or the next party and instead saw a great woman that was right in front of me.

After laundry we went back to the hotel. Rhino and I changed into swimwear and went down to the pool area while my dad took a nap. We brought our alcohol and were the only two in there.

"Dude, let's hop in the hot tub," I suggested.

"Right behind you."

I had just complained earlier that day about how much I hated beer, but Rhino's citrus beer proved to be rather tasty.

"This shit is good," I said, now on my third.

Beginning to get a buzz, I seized a photo opportunity to show-case my defined abs. Ever since I got them around the age of twenty I had always been proud of them. I relished every chance to show them off, specifically to women. It was the only part of my body that was noteworthy. Other than those six muscles, my body was skin and bone. It didn't matter if I ate Burger King for a week straight or organic bananas. My body always looked the same.

With this bravado, there were always detractors. "Skinny guys having abs are like fat chicks having big boobs," my good friend Jimmer told me in an attempt to tear me down. I always figured my abs were what made me unique. Like men with big biceps or women with long legs, we all have our specialties, and this was mine.

I started snapping photos, searching for just the right angle while dealing with limited light.

"Why are you always such a douche?" Rhino bemoaned.

"Will you take a photo?" I asked.

"Hell no!"

I finally got the right angle and lighting. I posted the photo to Facebook and instantly felt like a rock star. I always needed that validation, whether it be for my abs or my newfound attractive facial features. As much as it is an inferiority complex of mine, it should be understood that for most of my life, I was not attractive; people, or women, did not find me appealing. I spent the first twenty years of my life trying to get people to look at me. Like a flip of the proverbial switch, I became good looking overnight. It was a new luxury, being the subject of the gaze. It also made me feel powerful. It made me feel so in control that I never wanted to give it up.

Most people who are attractive have been that way their whole lives. I have been on both ends of the spectrum. I have been the ugly kid no one wanted to look at, and I've been the guy that every woman wanted to see. Not wanting to relinquish this power has ruined many of my relationships, mostly the one with Nicole. She was the best thing to ever happen to me, and I was too stupid to realize it. I'd talk to other women not only at bars but also on my phone, downloading dating apps whenever I went to work and was out of her sight. I was like a dog with a bone. I wanted that validation from other women; the same women I felt deprived me of it for so many years.

I became so wrapped up in my own universe and vanity that I neglected the first woman who ever loved me as who I was. Nicole loved me for my personality, not any superficial reason. She loved me for all the things I did before I was popular. She loved me for my intelligence and all the things I wanted to do in life. Even though she had spats of infidelity, I still loved her unconditionally. I didn't care that she had made mistakes. She was worth it. In the end, after choosing myself over her and our relationship, I lost her, and I received no validation because it left me with only loneliness and regret.

For dinner, the three of us decided that we wanted to have steak. It seemed a fitting meal for our last night. I Googled local steakhouses in Winnipeg, and up popped an array of options. A place called 529 Wellington was the closest to where we were.

"We might as well try to go to that one," said my dad.

On our way there, we entered a very upscale part of the city. Beautiful buildings and houses lined the roads. It was clear that this steakhouse was going to be one worth remembering. As my dad turned left onto the street where the steakhouse was located, no restaurants or signs popped up. I rapidly looked at my phone, then back at my GPS, trying to make sure I didn't miss our stop.

"Go slow," I kept saying to my dad.

"I can't go any slower. There are people behind me."

"What the hell?" I muttered to myself. "Where is this place?"

"Destination is on your right," said Siri.

Quickly my dad turned at the only turn available. I looked out the window and marveled at the building before me. It was a cream color, like a light piece of caramel. There was no sign indicating we had arrived at 529 Wellington. We sat parked in the lot for a few minutes until a few people walked in. We then knew we had to be at the right place.

They say you can never trust your GPS, and this time I could see why. Rocking my Target jeans and Minnesota Twins sweatshirt, I walked in first. Rhino was wearing a similar attire, as was my dad.

"Good evening, sir," a kind older man greeted me. "May I take your coat?"

I had on only my jacket that I wore for biking, so this gracious man had taken off perhaps the ugliest jacket he had ever seen.

Feeling out of place, I asked the man, "Is there a dress code to eat here?"

"No, sir. You gentlemen are perfectly fine."

To the left was a lounge filled with businessmen who were sipping on happy hour cocktails. My dad began scratching his head, embarrassed to be seen in his current clothes. My dad was a banker, so I understood his hesitation, but it wasn't like anyone from his bank was going to be there to chide him for his appearance.

"Would you gentlemen like to head to the lounge or be seated right away?" asked the host. We all looked at each other confused, clearly showing we had never been to a place of this status. "Let's just go to the dining room," he offered.

We were seated and shown a bevy of options for food and beverages. Our server, a roughly thirty-year-old man with a large belly and even larger knowledge of the menu, brought us each a pint of beer that he guaranteed we would love.

"I don't usually like beer," I told him.

"You'll like this one," he quickly responded. He was right. The beer was great. It was the best I've ever had, and they only brewed it in Winnipeg.

"I feel so out of place," said Rhino, looking around to see if anyone was looking at him.

A few men had taken up seats in the other dining room. There were only a couple of other people eating dinner where we were seated.

"This place is gorgeous," my dad opined.

The entrance was unique, with a stair set that led upstairs for large parties, a corridor that led somewhere else, and then glass doors that led to various dining rooms. Large paintings were displayed on every wall. A rustic, wooden siding with dark colors gave our room a prestigious feeling.

"How old is this place?" asked Rhino as he gulped down more beer.

"No idea," my dad and I said simultaneously.

"Quent, act more mature. You're behaving like you don't belong here," ordered my dad when he saw my puppy dog eyes wouldn't vanish.

"To be honest, I don't think I do belong here, Dad."

All of us looked around the room instead of talking to each other.

"What brings you gentlemen here this evening?" asked our waiter as he displayed different types of meat for each of us to choose from.

"We biked here from St. Cloud, Minnesota," I said.

"Holy cow. That's quite impressive. Are you guys professionals?"

"I like to think so," I said in a snide manner. My dad glared at me.

"How many miles is that?" asked the portly man.

"Roughly four hundred, sir. We are biking back tomorrow."

Each of us ordered a steak, by far the best I've ever tasted. The server attributed this taste to the fact that cows in Canada were grass fed. This steak was so good it didn't need A-1. By itself, this slab of meat made up for all the corn nuts and beef jerky I had been eating throughout the trip.

After our meal, we left, and the server and the host both wished us luck with the rest of our trip. The host tried to put my jacket back on for me. Since I had never experienced this type of service before, I looked like a weirdo trying to put one arm in one sleeve before the other.

"Can you tell I've never done this before?" I asked the host, his frustration turning into a grin.

I took a photo of 529 Wellington before we entered the car. This place was a treat, and if we had done our due diligence on finding a steakhouse, we never would have ended up there. Sometimes it does pay off to trust your GPS.

Later that night, we went to the MTS Centre where the Winnipeg Jets of the NHL played hockey. They had a road game that night, but the bar was still packed with patrons who combined food and alcohol with their viewing experience. Once again, the drinks were intolerable. It got so bad, I wondered aloud if we could bring our own alcohol into the restaurant.

"I'll pay them to let me bring my own bottle in here," I deadpanned.

An older man, likely my father's age, sat down directly next to him. In America, it is considered creepy to sit right next to someone in a bar if there are other options for seating. Yet this stranger was unabashed in his approach. He quickly struck up a conversation with my father about hockey and how he thought it was the most peculiar sport he had ever witnessed. For context, the man was of middle-Eastern descent, so hockey was probably something he was unaccustomed with.

Rhino managed his cell phone, which he had been deprived of for days until my dad stopped by our place in St. Cloud to pick it up. For Rhino, it must have felt like centuries since he had his phone. He was always on it, looking for great deals on Groupon or for his next date on Bumble.

On this night, Rhino could not get enough of the bar we were at. The exotic lighting and blue walls gave the place a vibrant look. There was a casino attached to the bar, a place the middle-Eastern man eventually gravitated toward after his conversation with my dad fizzled out. Rhino's Snap Story (a component of Snapchat) was filled with him twirling his camera around as he showed his virtual friends how much fun he was having. At one point, he put his massive phone in my face and bellowed "Q! Say hello to my little friend!" I blamed the alcohol for his clichéd sentiment, but hey, at least the guy was having a good time.

My dad and I transitioned into a conversation I will never forget. We talked about our sexuality, and how each of us had exploited our desires respectively. Rhino would later go on to say it was the weirdest exchange he had ever overheard.

"You know, there are things that I have never told your mom about my past. She and I have kept it pretty closed."

"See, for me, I like to talk about that kind of stuff. I think it gives me a new perspective on someone," I said.

"You and Nicole talk about that stuff?" my dad asked.

"To an extent. My previous thing with that chick from St. Bens was a disaster because all she talked about was her ex. I don't do that with Nicole. She and I just talk about the past to feel each other out."

"Does she know how many women you have slept with?" my dad asked. "Twenty? Thirty? Fifty? You must be at some crazy number."

"Somewhere around there," I told him, careful not to reveal the actual number or the fact that I had not told Nicole.

"How many guys has she been with?"

"Not that many. Like four, I think."

"Really!" replied my father, flabbergasted.

"It's not that many at all, Dad."

"Well, back in my day . . ."

"You have to be kidding me. You actually think four is a high number?"

"I do."

I didn't understand why my dad was so surprised. It showed how socialized we are to expect our men to be highly sexual and women to not behave in that manner. It is really sad because women get unfairly judged for acts like that. A woman is just as sexual as a man is, no matter how much society is conditioned to think otherwise. I personally felt Nicole was rather conservative with her sexual past, but when my dad thought it was a lot, I could only laugh and shake my head. The generational gap could not have been more apparent.

"Seriously though, Dad. I feel like that part of my life is over. I'm happy with Nicole. I think I simply needed to experience some things before I met her."

"I hope that works out for you," my dad said, shaking his head thinking Nicole would leave me once she knew.

I had meant to tell Nicole, but she never asked. I felt embarrassed to tell her because when she told me her number, I knew we hadn't shared the same turbulent past. Yet I didn't want to lose her over something I considered no big deal.

Eventually I did tell her. We were in my room and she was looking at a poster of a scantily clad woman I had plastered on my wall. She walked over to it and, for whatever reason, further examined it.

"Are their checkmarks on this woman's underwear?" she questioned.

I was done for. "There are, but they're from a long time ago."

"What do they mean?"

It was judgment day and I had to 'fess up. "Each line stands for one woman I've slept with."

Nicole counted the check marks. "Well, now I know how many people you have slept with."

The poster was always something I prided myself on. It was something I could look at during the night and reflect on each experience if I was feeling lonely. Once I met Nicole, I took a marker and colored over the check marks to hide my idiocy. It worked for the longest time until that day, when she noticed my coloring pattern didn't match the rest of the poster.

I sat on my bed, my face as red as Ragu, unable to look at Nicole while I frantically searched the floor for a hole to bury myself in.

"It's okay," she finally said, relieving me of my past and showing that she loved me regardless. I nearly broke down in tears. I wasn't embarrassed about my number. I didn't think it was that high. Yet when I saw Nicole's reaction, I knew my past had come back to haunt me.

This conversation I had with my dad was an important one for more than one reason. The lack of acceptance of the sexualized woman in western societies still plagues us. It is a plague that does not allow for more growth and progression. As mentioned, our men are glamorized for their sexual conquests, while women are shamed for their endeavors. This disconnect, simply put, stems from our media and pop culture influences. The man, despite the lessening of this effect in recent decades, is still the target of our entertainment. His gaze dominates our advertising, film, television, etc. These forms of media are designed with his best interests in mind. We will not have a chance for more equality between the genders if this gaping reality is not changed. Unfortunately, this gap will have to be narrowed both politically and socially, which is something that will not happen unless both men and women alike acknowledge the injustice that occurs in society.

This dialogue was also important because my dad and I had never talked about something so serious before. Usually the only times we reached these deep heartfelt moments was if he told me I had to try harder in school or to stop being such a rude person toward my mom. After this, he and I had a new perspective on each other. He knew more about me, and I more about him, for better or worse.

After the heavy conversation, and a few more nonsatiating drinks, we drove back to the hotel. We watched an atrocious John Cusack movie. It was one of the better movie options on pay-per-view, but the entire viewing experience consisted of Rhino occasionally leaving to go smoke a cigarette and my dad telling me how important the next day was going to be.

My knees had been killing me for the last few days. My back had softened up, but my knees and the muscles above them were tenser than Game 7 of the NBA Finals. The discomfort was so bad that at one point during my sleep I reached to grab at my right knee, only I wound up grabbing my dad's knee instead. I massaged the knee for a few moments, thinking it was my own. It wasn't until my dad grabbed my hand and threw it away did I realize that the pleasure my knee felt wasn't actually happening. Unlike our conversation earlier in the night, this topic was never brought up.

Knowing that the next day we would be leaving Winnipeg and heading back home sunk in when I woke up with a hot flash for what seemed like the eleventh time that night. It was a journey back that would be filled with much less fanfare, yet a journey that was as integral to the adventure as the first half. Part of me wanted to just hop in the car and get a ride all the way back, but there was a small voice hidden deep in my brain that implored me to keep going. It would be too easy to sit back and be satisfied with what we had done. It would be more impressive to finish what we had set out to do. Four days and three nights. That is what stood between our everyday lives and something more profound.

CHAPTER THIRTEEN

We awoke the next morning and prepared to leave Canada. I went downstairs to the front desk to borrow a toothbrush for the third day in a row. We had clean clothes, not much of a hangover, courtesy of Canadian protocol, and a ride toward five miles of the border.

Walking out to the car, a dejected emotion overcame me. I genuinely did not want to be in Winnipeg anymore, but I also realized that upon my departure, I would be leaving a part of me there. So much of the past four months had been devoted to conjuring up a plan to get to Winnipeg. Leaving, the reality was that it was now over. In a sense, the dream had come and gone. Rhino and I were now merely riding for each other to get back to a place that had no new significance.

With that being said, I don't know if I ever want to come back to Winnipeg.

"I could see myself living here," were Rhino's thoughts on the city.

Still for me, Winnipeg was a place of accomplishment. It was a place I went to find something about myself, not to lose myself.

We fetched our bikes from the storage container and carried our gear out to the back where my dad's van was located. Many cars were plugged into outlets.

"That's so the car batteries don't freeze overnight," my dad informed us.

We turned left out of the parking lot, the hotel now literally and figuratively in the rearview mirror. At a gas station, my dad filled up with enough gas to hopefully get him all the way back to Osseo. The drive to the drop off point was as expected. It was like South Dakota, in that you travel through miles upon miles of vast, open land until you finally run into something.

"Great faces, no fucking places," as my friend Jason once said.

It was the last time for a while that I would see kilometers on the speed limit sign. It was the last time I would be on Canadian soil for the foreseeable future. This myriad of emotions regarding all the abstractness is one of the truly beautiful things in life because it all comes together in an indescribable way. I later tried to tell someone what I was feeling at that moment and usually I came up with terms like, "It's hard to say" or "I don't even know." Perhaps ignorance is bliss in this type of situation, and what I feel in these moments should not be analyzed but rather enjoyed at surface level and cherished because that feeling will never come again.

We arrived at our drop-off point, a few miles short of the border.

"I'm going to miss you, Dad," I said, knowing I would see him again but becoming emotional regardless.

I thanked him for everything that he did in the last few days, and not just financially. During that span, we had grown closer and explored different subjects I never thought we would. It was a period of time I will never forget because it was one of the rare moments where my dad wasn't my dad. He was my friend, someone I could share experiences and talk with about anything. The next time I would see him, he would merely be Dad again, which made this trip and this moment all the more memorable.

We then began our way back. Our day would only be a forty-five-mile ride. Once we crossed the border, we would return to Karlstad at a relatively decent hour. In twenty minutes, we pulled up to the check in station. There was no exhilaration or excitement this time. It was just something we had to do to get back to the country where we resided. They let us through without much questioning. I halfheartedly hoped they would drag us into an interrogation room, just to add some intrigue to the event.

We were now stateside and off to Karlstad. We would have a few stops in between, if needed, but other than that, we were right back out there with nature, away from urbanized society. It was apparent Rhino didn't want to be out there. I think he was tired of it all. I don't blame him because I was in the same state, emotionally. So we just rode next to each other silently. Like I mentioned, we went through so much hardship just to get to Winnipeg. Now having to do all that again just to return to St. Cloud, it was easy to see why there was no energy between us.

After I could bear the silence no more, I again prodded him on his love life.

"Why are you asking me that again?" he wondered. "You know I don't talk about that."

"Bro, come on. Give me something to work with here. I'm not trying to die of boredom before we get to dead-ass Karlstad."

I needed something to put some pep into our collective step. This day would be very manageable. This was a day to get back into rhythm. It was the next days we had to be concerned about. We had a 91-mile day, 105-mile day, and then our last day was planned to be 98 miles. Today's 45-mile jaunt would be cake compared to those days. We arrived back in Karlstad around dinnertime.

We checked back into the same motel, where the older woman who had helped us earlier greeted us with a surprised look.

"I didn't know if you two were going to make good on your reservation."

I'm sure she thought that we would either be eaten by a bear or run off the road and be left for dead. Yet here we were, in her presence, ready for a room for the night.

It was still light outside, so Rhino and I decided to do what we do best: drink. The older woman told us about the American Legion, so we walked for a mile to a three-way stop to sit down for a couple of adult beverages. There was your typical day crowd in there, but no one that looked like they wanted to be a nuisance.

We sat down and hammered down drinks rapidly. Rhino splurged on SoCo 7s and I found myself drinking Crown and Coke because they didn't carry Grey Goose. This was now the second time on the trip that I drank something new. I slowly learned that one day there could be a life outside of Grey Goose. We each had a few shots of Fireball and Rum Chata. By the last shot, I was getting drunk.

"Another round of those please," Rhino said to the bartender.

"Can I get more Rum Chata than Fireball in mine?" I embarrassingly asked.

"What the fuck?" Rhino said in his usual grumpy tone.

We had been at the bar for a couple hours now. We had seen an older bartender with glasses who was passing out shots of whiskey get replaced by a younger, better looking blonde woman. Of course my decision was met with jeers from Rhino and an emasculating look from the new bartender. Rhino then berated me for ten minutes about how much more of a man he was because of how much he could drink. It reminded me of the conversation we had back in Winnipeg where Rhino digressed on how great the Packers were. That talk led me wanting to punch him in the face and annihilate what was left of his balding head.

This time, I just let him talk. I let him have his moment. I was simply happy we were together. I was joyed that we were doing what we set out to do. For as much contention as we understandably had throughout the trip, we also were both mature enough to recognize that it was inevitable. What was said or done on our journey was not personal, but rather just a natural reaction to the physical, mental, and emotional stress we were enduring.

After his tirade, a man approached us. He introduced himself and later revealed that he, along with his mother, were owners of the motel we were staying at. He was a gracious, pleasant man. He had a genuine interest in what we were doing and wanted to know all about our journey. Most people in these settings talk to each other to be polite or for their own personal benefit. With this man, he merely wanted to get to know two people who were staying at his business.

"Where are you guys originally from?" he asked.

"Independence, Wisconsin," said Rhino.

"Osseo, down by the cities. It's just a little town smack dab in the middle of a bunch of other larger cities."

"Yes, I have been to Osseo. Nice little town," the man said.

We talked about many things with this man, including the difference between living in cities compared to the country, the political climate of our country, and any other topic that usually presents itself during small talk. More than anything, this man just wanted to talk to us. He just wanted to see us as people. I imagine Karlstad doesn't see many new people passing through, so Rhino and I walking into the American Legion during the middle of the day most likely captivated his interest.

An hour passed, and sensing our conversation was nearing its conclusion, he stood up to leave. While doing so, he picked up both of our tabs.

"Sir, you don't have to do that," I said.

"No, I want to. You guys are giving us some business so I just want to say thank you."

I didn't know what to say to this man, so I said nothing. His generosity was too much. Our tabs weren't exorbitant, but it was the principle of his gesture that was so impactful.

"Damn, he's a nice guy," Rhino observed.

Having our demeanors lifted, we exited and headed back. I could barely walk straight because I had drank too much. We walked through a small neighborhood, simply enjoying being in a different part of the world. I stopped to take a video of Rhino jumping in the snow, which was becoming more of a rare sight as we moved further into March.

"It's great to be back in America!" he yelled as he launched himself into a mound of black snow. It was safe to say he was hammered.

I told Rhino I'd meet him at the motel and then veered off to a small thrift shop, hoping to find a small souvenir for Nicole. I told her I would get her something while I was gone, but with everything it had slipped my mind. I was determined to make good on my promise to her.

"My daughter just moved to St. Cloud," said an older woman working behind the counter. "I hope the gangs aren't as bad as they say they are."

"Don't worry, ma'am. There aren't too many problems in Cloud, unless you go looking for trouble."

I walked around the store for ten minutes. It all seemed like junk. It was another reminder of why I hate shopping. I used to think I hated it because my mom would drag me around J. C. Penney three times a week when I was a young boy, but the older I became, I learned I genuinely hate shopping. It's why I always know what I want before I go to the store.

I was close to giving up when I stumbled upon a pair of socks that had Karlstad printed on them. I figured they would look cute on Nicole's tiny feet. I also bought her a necklace that I later almost forgot to take the tag off of before I gave it to her. If she would have seen the eight dollar sticker, that might have given her more impetus to leave me.

At this point, my funds were minimal. I had to pay for the motel that night, plus the one in Clearbrook the following night. All things considered, I had about $150 to work on for food, booze, and whatever other nuisance might pop up in the next couple of days.

I went back to the motel to pay for our room. Rhino joined me in the office and we chatted with the older woman for a few minutes.

"You know what? You guys can go in to the liquor store and take whatever you want," she said as we were preparing to go back to the room.

"Oh no, ma'am. Your son just . . ."

"I know. Please, don't be bashful. Go and take something."

The store wasn't that big, but it didn't have to be. I looked at the bottle of Grey Goose and reached for it. Before I touched it, I pulled back my hand. It would have been extremely selfish of me to take that bottle; not only because it was expensive but also because there was no way I could bring it back with me. I opted for a large can of Mike's Hard Lemonade.

I began to feel teary eyed. "Thank you so much. Seriously, this is so nice of you two. It really is a testament to how classy your family is. Also, I again want to apologize for the whole key incident. I ended up finding it in my pocket."

The older woman laughed. "Go on. You two need some rest."

I simply could not make sense of what just happened. Her son had already paid our whole bar tab, and now she gave us even more free liquor. It was not the free liquor that nearly brought me to tears but rather the genuine care she showed for us. It went to show that fantastic people come from all corners of the earth. She and her son's generosity left a lasting impression on me. The North Star Motor Inn in Karlstad, Minnesota, will always have a soft spot in my heart, most of which I attribute to two of the most selfless people I have had the pleasure of meeting.

CHAPTER FOURTEEN

The following morning, I was a little groggy from the previous night's happenings, but more than ready to get back out there. My knees and lumbar had partially recovered in the few days of not riding and then the sole day of minimal riding. Still, I could feel an everlasting strain that would be with me for the duration of our journey. This was more mental than physical. I knew my body would be able to handle the tugs and pulls at every muscle, but my mind would have to weather being pulled in different directions. It would be easy now to call days short. Not many people outside of our close friends and family were invested in the ride anymore. Not having this superficiality to use for motivation added even more to the fact that Rhino and I were riding for each other above all else.

"Rhino, get up."

"Ten more minutes."

He was feeling the ramifications of the previous night. This was evident as we began riding. He simply wasn't functioning like he needed to be. Rhino wasn't slowing me down, but it was apparent that he needed some time to get into a rhythm. We were fifteen miles in and the day was not very old. It was right then that I knew we had a great chance to get to Clearbrook without any assistance.

I had by now distanced myself from Rhino when I decided to stop at a Cenex gas station, where I had a quick chat with a gentleman we had briefly met at the Cenex in Brooks.

"I didn't think I would ever see you guys again," he remarked. "You go that far north and something bad is bound to happen."

I went outside and waited for twenty minutes with Bruce, who had gotten an early start to his day.

"Is Ryan hungover?"

"He might be, Bruce. We drank quite a bit yesterday," trying not to throw one of my best friends under the bus.

"Well, that's what he gets for drinking like that."

I nibbled on a breakfast burrito and waited for a small figure to appear. The road we were on spanned miles in both directions. Soon Rhino became larger and larger, finally able to catch up.

"How are we feeling, Rhino?" I said in a sarcastic tone.

"I need an energy drink and an orange juice," he replied, walking into the gas station hurriedly.

"I don't know how today is going to go, Bruce. He's going to have to be better than this."

"He'll feel better soon enough. Q, I'm going to go to Thief River and meet up with you guys there. We can get lunch or something."

Rhino consumed his beverages at a slow pace.

"Bro, I know you're not feeling the best, but we have a good shot of making it all the way today," I said, trying to be encouraging.

"I'm fine. Just a little hungover. Let's get back out there."

We crossed over a large horizon while the sun beat down on us. This occurrence reaffirmed that we were going to make it. When we made the left turn into Thief River, thirty miles away from Karlstad, we still had momentum. Rhino was riding at a better pace. We agreed to meet at the Dawg House for lunch. It seemed like an interesting enough place on the way through to warrant stopping.

I was a few minutes ahead of Rhino so I decided to order a Grey Goose to keep my good vibes intact. I managed to drink half of it by the time he arrived, but he saw what I had done.

"What are you drinking?" he hastily requested.

"A water . . . and a Grey Goose."

"I'm feeling icky and you order a drink. Man, you are one weird bird. Have a little respect."

The latter half of my drink wasn't as enjoyable after his complaint registered. I didn't feel bad about drinking. I had indulged the previous day but not to the point where it would affect the next day.

"It's just one, bro. Chill." I said in defense.

"Yeah. But my dad is going to pay for this meal, so in a way you are kind of using him."

"Rhino, how much shit did my dad buy you? It will all work itself out."

I kept looking behind me out the window to make sure our bikes were still there. It would have been upsetting if one or both of us had our bikes stolen.

We were again diligent in getting out of the restaurant in a reasonable fashion. Our pace was right where it needed to be on this day, making spending too long at lunch hard to justify. The wind had shifted directions from the first time through and was again on our backs. For our sixth day of riding, it was a welcome relief that I embraced to no end. It would be another thirty miles until we reached the gas station in Brooks. Getting to Brooks by 2:00 to 3:00 p.m. would leave us ample time to adjust our pace to whatever was necessary for a smooth last stretch.

There seemed to be this tension building between Rhino and I during the time from Thief River Falls to Brooks, mostly because I rode so far in front of him. It was evident that he could not keep the pace that I was pushing, and I was frustrated because I didn't know if he was taking his sweet time or physically struggling. I love Rhino like a brother, but I still couldn't believe he was so far behind me.

Ten miles in, I stopped to check my phone, knowing he was at least two miles behind. He had called, so I called him back. He didn't answer. There was no time to waste; not with this wind favoring us like it was. I stopped a few miles later to stretch out my legs and saw that he called again. We were in a classic game of phone tag, neither of us willing to leave a voicemail. This was an asinine decision on both parts because we were in an unfamiliar area where if one of us got hurt, we wouldn't have a semblance of an idea where the other was.

It has to be understood that I couldn't just sit on the side of the highway and wait for Rhino. He was a good two to three miles behind, so to wait for him would have taken twenty minutes. Waiting wouldn't have been the end of the world, but I could not wait and let my body tighten up. Again, this was a moment that needed to be exploited. It was very possible that when we turned left off the highway, the wind would be against us in a negative way.

I was putting miles behind me as cars raced by my beat-up jacket and dirt-ridden bicycle. After another ten miles, I took one last stretch break and checked my phone. My back was hollering at me to take a pause. My knees felt like the equivalent of an old man trying to climb eight sets of stairs. Rhino had finally left a voicemail telling me to wait for him at the Cenex gas station in Brooks.

"I'm feeling better. Just wait for me at the gas station," he said.

I was going to wait for him regardless. Still, it struck me as a plea for forgiveness. Rhino knew he was letting me down, but with his hard-natured, unrelenting personality, he would never admit as much.

A few miles later, I saw the sign that directed me to head west back toward Clearbrook. It's these types of mini moments throughout a day that you live for as a biker. It's like pulling up your bank account and realizing that you didn't spend as much money as you initially anticipated at the bars the night prior, so you decide you can go out again the next night. I wheeled into the Cenex, ready to wait for as long as it took Rhino to show.

The last time I was there, it was more eventful because of the small gathering that had formed around Bruce to listen to him gush about our adventure. On this occasion, I didn't even bother going into the store. A weird feeling overcame me. I felt guilty about what I had done to one of my best friends and worried for his safety, but he knew what he signed up for on this trip. It was just like when he left me on the same exact route when I was struggling with my lower back pain. For as much as bicycling is a team activity, you are, in a sense, also by yourself. The trip would have been just as hard had we been neck and neck the whole way.

Twenty minutes later, he finally pulled up. His arrival justified my decision to leave him behind, but this justification had to be internalized.

"Thanks for waiting," he said in a snarky manner.

I didn't try to rationalize with him. I knew that attempt would be futile because he was upset with how his ride was going and his personality would not allow for him to show any kind of weakness.

It really is sad how fragile the male ego is. Countless times we are expected to be strong-willed, relentless individuals, but there are also moments that we have to break down and, if we are unable to cry, at least sit there and try exhibit emotion. I personally don't buy into the belief that society is unforgiving of its male's emotionality. I don't feel ostracized when I have an emotion that I need to address, whether that is with a male or female conversationalist. I think, if anything, society is too hard on our females for their oftentimes overt displays of emotion. I suppose that is why a man crying is so hard to comprehend, because we find managing one gender's display of emotions too taxing as is.

This isn't to suggest that Rhino went inside the bathroom and started bawling his eyes out. He just had to reset because with only thirty miles left, we were in an advantageous position. This day, however easy my riding may have been, was still going to take us for all we were worth.

When Rhino returned from inside, he was in a better mood. He probably did some self-reflecting and decided that life is just too short to hold any grudges, especially since we were stuck together for the last few days. The time we had spent together was beginning to manifest in contempt, as expected. Again, it likely originated at the bar in Winnipeg when we were getting heated talking about the Packers. Since then we had some fantastic times, but that spat laid the groundwork for future conflict.

We started off quiet as we began to set the pace leaving Brooks.

"Let's just take our time, bro. We have plenty of time before the sun goes down," I noted.

I rode alongside Rhino, and it wasn't out of pity. I lost my momentum when I was waiting for him at the gas station. My muscles had begun to seize up again, and all I wanted to do was use the extra daylight to navigate our path in an easy yet productive fashion.

The seven-mile stretch away from Brooks was nothing like the seven-mile stretch there, fortunately. This time there was no unrelenting wind in our face, and it didn't take us over an hour to travel seven miles. We rode the stretch as if we were going out for a quick stroll before sunset.

When we finished the stretch, Rhino turned and said, "Wow, that was easier."

We were a few minutes into that turn when danger suddenly appeared, this time in the form of a pack of dogs. Unlike in Brainerd, these dogs were nasty. I turned to my left and saw a pack of seven in a parallel junkyard come rushing at us. There was a fence encasing the junkyard. We picked up our pace, but there was no panic setting in. As soon as I thought that we were safe, a gaping hole in the fence twenty yards ahead appeared. One by one, each dog made its way through the fence. I looked around and saw that there was no one else around. These dogs were rabid and wild. I began pedaling as fast as I could. I looked back to see the closest dog was about ten feet away. All the pain and soreness that I was feeling was quickly replaced by adrenaline as I pedaled as hard as at any moment of our trip.

"Dude, go!" I yelled at Rhino, who was to my left.

I felt stuck in time. I could only go so fast. I thought at least one or two dogs were going to catch either of us. I continued to pump my legs as hard as I could. This was why I spent so many long hours in the gym, for moments that called for superior proficiency. If I lost footing on one of my pedals, or if my pace slowed, I could have been attacked.

Gradually, the dogs began to back off as we separated ourselves. Rhino and I turned to each other, as if to say, "Wow, *that* wasn't easy."

From there, our dialogue intensified. Perhaps still feeling the adrenaline from earlier, I grilled him more about a past fling of his, Britta.

"Can we talk about Britta now?"

"What do you want to know?"

"Something. Just give me something to hold on to, Rhino."

"All right, I got a story for you." My eyes lit up. "So back when I was playing baseball in Weed, California, I had a friend I always used to smoke pot with. Well, over winter break, we went back to Independence and, at one point, hung out with Britta and her friend." Then Rhino stopped talking.

"Um. Is that the story?" I asked.

"No, obviously. I had a snowflake stuck in my mouth."

"Continue then."

"Well, we are hanging out, and Britta wants to get after it, so we go to her car. Well, while that was going on, my friend and her friend went into her car, and well, you can use your imagination."

I loved it. Every part of his story gave me more perspective on who he was. For the longest time, I thought Rhino was asexual, but this small blip into his personal life allowed me to relate to him so much better.

"Bro, that might be one of the better stories you have ever told me, and not just because it was about Britta," I said in a thankful manner.

I had met Britta a few months back and could see the attraction he had for her. Rhino was my boy, so of course I wanted to know more about her. My roommates and I always grilled Rhino about her, probing him for answers he clearly didn't want to give. She was a really nice girl, so why he was so against talking about her I'll never know. I tie it back to the fact that men, in general, aren't highly capable of expressing their feelings.

Men are good with rhetoric when they are attempting to pick a girl up from a bar or are having a heated discussion about sports. After that, most of us can barely articulate what we had for dinner two nights prior. It extends to the writing or texting realm of communication as well.

Let's take the dating app Tinder for example. Here, there is not a whole lot of pressure. The way the app works is that for communication to ever happen, both parties have to, simply put, acknowledge that they find each other titillating. It is a tad more complex than that but not too much. With that being said, even though the pressure is now somewhat off the male because his vanity is being appealed to, he still at times finds a way to come off as a brainless fool. Some women will argue that they take the initiative to message men first, and this is true, but more commonly men are the instigators of dialogue.

This is perhaps why so many people confuse androgyny with metrosexuality. This is conceited but also a positive indictment of the power of liberal arts degrees. I have a way with words, and Tinder is the perfect app for someone of my talents. Tinder, in my opinion, is so much more than just posing sexually charged yes or no questions to your matches. Tinder is a way to showcase your personality before ever meeting someone in a face-to-face setting. Typically I have the ability to engage women in thought-provoking, scintillating conversation. This isn't to say that I am better or smarter than other men, but simply more willing to be vulnerable and explore deep recesses of the English language that plays out in an advantageous manner. If only my dialogue with Rhino on the subject of Britta was always as rewarding as a night of steamy conversation on an iPhone. This time was different though, and I was thankful to be there for it.

We didn't know it until then, but we were making incredible progress. We were only fifteen miles away from Clearbrook, so we stopped for what we hoped would be our last break. Our pace was steady, but nothing like on the way to Brooks. Still, it was only five in the afternoon. With any luck, we would be pulling into Clearbrook in about ninety minutes.

As we commenced, my body began to tire. My legs were starting to tighten up and my whole upper body desired to be parallel with the rest of my body again. I had to call another break after a few miles. I couldn't get the soreness out of my knees and lower back. I wanted to get to Clearbrook quickly, but not at the cost of making tomorrow and the last day difficult.

We stopped one more time and now the wind was beginning to pick up. It wasn't going to kill us, but it would slow us down. As we were stopped, I sucked into my water bottle, squeezing the most I could of the liquid that hadn't froze.

Suddenly a car whizzed by, and seconds later my bike slowly fell over to the ground. I reached for it but came up short in my fragile state. I didn't think anything of it other than to curse the wind another hundred times.

We started moving along, and all of a sudden, I started hearing a clicking nose emanating from my back tire. Our pace hadn't suffered, so I assumed it was the wind or some other force. We veered west a tad more and had the winds almost on our backs again. We were flying, but the noise from the rear of my bike hadn't faded. If anything, it worsened.

"Rhino, do you see anything going on with my back tire?"

He looked and came up empty. "It seems to be moving just fine." Again, neither Rhino nor myself knew the first thing about bike maintenance, besides putting air in the tires. I progressively became more worried as the sound didn't stop. I was riding very well, so there seemed no reason to make a move until we got to the hotel.

The miles continued to click off as we neared our destination. It seemed that whenever there was an outside force threatening our ride, we somehow rode better. The noise on the back of my bike was bothering me, but I only rode more efficiently because of it.

Pulling into Clearbrook, we passed another horse-drawn carriage and the Tesoro gas station where we ate breakfast. It was a Friday night in Clearbrook. A Friday night there was like a Monday night in St. Cloud. Yet the town had a buzz to it that I cannot accurately put into words.

We went to a diner and had a chicken dinner. The other patrons and some of the employees sensed we were not from around the area, but no words were exchanged on the subject. I turned to Rhino and looked at him. He had gulped down a few Miller Lites and looked to be at peace. I hate speculating, but if he was indeed still suffering through a hangover, I don't understand why he would want to drink derelict beer.

We quietly exited the bar and drove back to the hotel. There wasn't anything going on, so we said good night to Bruce and sat in the hotel. A North Carolina–Notre Dame basketball game was on. It was March, so the annual March Madness was captivating the nation. College basketball didn't do too much for me anymore. I used to really enjoy it, but ever since high school, my affinity slowly waned.

To compound my emotional state, I had diagnosed the buzzing noise from earlier. A spoke on my bike was out of place and my brake pads were dislodged. At this point, fear struck me again. I wondered how I would ever get my bike ready to ride in such a short period. I called my dad.

"Dad, my brakes seem to be out of alignment."

"What do you mean?"

"Well, I mean the back part of my brakes are kind of disconnected and now my wheel won't rotate."

"Use the tool set I put in your bag."

"Dad, you know I'm not going to be able to do that."

"Quent, at least try. No, send me pictures of it and I'll think of something."

I realized I had probably ruined his evening TV schedule, but I needed my dad's help. Soon after, he called me back.

"Okay, I know what's wrong. Here is what you need to do," and then rambled off a novel's worth of instructions, none of which resonated.

"Dad. Go slower. That's too much right away."

I started banging at the brake pad with a tool and nothing was happening. I did many forms of this practice for some time before giving up.

"Dad, I'll have to call you back."

My dad was very good at fixing bikes, but not very good at being patient with me. I can't blame him. Here he was trying to help me out from hundreds of miles away and all I could do was listen helplessly as he instructed me what to do. I asked Rhino for some help, but he was more worthless than me. My dad at one point had asked if Bruce could help, and I regrettably laughed because I knew there was no way Bruce would be coming to the rescue on this one.

I never called my dad back that night. I had all sorts of tools laid out in front of me, but they might as well not have been there. I told my dad I would call him back, but in reality I was going to make a few more half-assed attempts at fixing it and then pout.

Rhino was still lying in bed, watching the game, and not being much support. I couldn't blame him, considering I wasn't much support to him hours earlier.

For as active as I am, I'm also incredibly lazy and horrible with mechanical problems. I would rather pay one hundred dollars to have someone change my tire than learn how to do it myself. AAA is a great resource, but if they weren't around to save me, I think it'd be more likely that I would sit in a ditch waiting for help than actually trying to fix the problem myself.

One night the previous winter, I was out with some woman. The roads were icy and I was trying to impress her by driving fast. I approached a downward turn and spun out. My car banged off the right sidewalk and then slid and rammed into the left curb.

I sat in my car, looking helpless in front of my date.

"How about that for adventure?" I casually joked.

In the morning, my tire had popped.

"Can't you change it?" she asked.

"I don't know how," I responded. Her eyes rolled all the way back to my room, along with the rest of her.

I called a towing company and paid seventy-five dollars to have them put on my spare tire. Not only did I lose seventy-five dollars, but the woman I had spent the previous night with never talked to me again.

I'm not ergonomically inept because I have no discernable skills. I could have probably fixed the tire in either of these situations if I really wanted to, but the truth is that kind of work eats at my soul. I just don't want to do it. It's the same reason why I failed so many math and science classes. I could have studied harder and learned enough of the material to pass the class, but again I would rather not make that effort. I still don't know if this laziness will kill me or set me behind in life.

The next time I looked at Rhino, he was well on his way to falling asleep.

"Rhino, we are going to have to drive to Bemidji tomorrow. My bike is busted and they're the only town that has a shop around here."

"Fuck. Fine," he said, and then went to sleep.

I did the same. It was getting late and I could barely keep my eyes open anymore. *It will all be better in the morning*, I thought.

CHAPTER FIFTEEN

Bruce was indifferent when we told him about the situation. "I suppose I can bring you guys to Bemidji." He knew what had to be done, so we piled our bikes into the back and headed for the only town close enough that had a chance for assistance. I looked on my phone and confirmed that Bemidji had one bike shop, fortunately. I called and there was no answer. I didn't tell Rhino because I thought he would become more upset if we had to drive further south.

We pulled into Bemidji and stopped at Denny's for breakfast. I was hungry but didn't really want to go in. We were getting closer to home, and I thought someone might recognize us and wonder why weren't outside riding.

I looked around the restaurant as Rhino and his dad's conversation about their family faded into the back of my mind. The restaurant had a lot of old people, and not many younger people like I expected, being that we were in a college town. It put me in a sour mood and provoked me to order a milkshake. This was one of the less pragmatic decisions of the journey because I knew as soon as we started riding I would have a gut-wrenching stomachache. I slurped down a few swigs and then apologized to Bruce because I assumed he was going to pay for our meal. I apologized again for assuming he was going to pay for our meal.

We left the restaurant and I called the bike shop again. This time there was an answer and the man that I was speaking to told me that their shop didn't do bike repairs anymore. My heart sank for a few seconds.

"But there is a place on the other side of town, and I know they're open," he assured me.

I called them and they gladly agreed to help me out. After the call, I noticed Rhino was Snapchatting Scooter. I knew that Scooter was going to see us inside the car and right away berate us. As predicted, a few minutes passed, and Rhino received a not-so-nice reply from him.

"Why are you guys in the car? I knew you weren't going to get every mile."

"Q's bike broke down, you idiot," Rhino fired back.

Rhino trying to explain our dilemma to Scooter over Snapchat was a wreck.

"Dude, there is no way you can explain the situation in ten seconds," I urged from the back seat.

We stopped at a gas station to fill up our packs. I purchased a few water bottles and a couple cheese crackers. The idea was to pack for the day so that we could make up for the lost time. We then went to the bike shop and walked in with my busted brake apparatus.

The men in the bike shop were very friendly, and when I told them of our story, they were part shocked, part thrilled to be able to help in this way.

"You guys really went all the way to Winnipeg?" asked the younger, friendlier one of the two.

"Yes. It was tough, but here we are," I said.

"That's crazy. So yeah, your bike should be ready in a half hour."

Another man came in and began talking to the storeowners about the Paul Bunyan Trail, a route we elected not to take going north because of the snow.

"I was just out there today and it has some snow, but nothing you can't ride over," the man announced.

I interjected. "Sir, if you don't mind me asking, how far did you go on the trail?"

"About twenty miles."

I went back to the car to talk to Rhino. "My bike will be done in twenty minutes or so, and I just talked to a guy who said the trail is clear for at least thirty miles," I exaggerated, trying to get Rhino to think about taking the trail.

"No doubt. We don't have to go back on the highway then," Rhino responded.

It was nearing noon and I was beginning to get anxious. The nice man said that they were almost done, and he rang me up for a discounted price.

"You don't have to do that," I said.

"My treat. I want to see the rest of your journey go well."

"Out of curiosity, what was wrong with my bike?" I asked.

The man went into a discourse on brake essentials and how that affected the tire, all material I didn't grasp.

"That makes perfect sense," I lied, and took my bike, which had been wheeled out to me.

I was fortunate that this shop was open, or much less existed. I exited the bike shop knowing we caught a break. When I called my dad to let him know how we planned to continue, he shared the same thought.

"You are lucky. Try your best to make sure it doesn't fall over again. That probably rattled the gears."

Bruce left and told us to meet him in Walker. As I began to stretch, my body was not responding well. Physically, the previous day was so great for me that I think on this day water found its level and my body reacted less kindly. My lumbar was in so many knots it would have made the Rubik's cube look simple. My knees were sore to the point where it affected my walking. The same could be said for my shoulders. I hated the feeling. The masculine-obsessed side of me refused to divulge this information to Rhino.

What I really needed was a day off or a very powerful muscle relaxer, but that wasn't going to happen. We set out and weaved through downtown Bemidji looking for signs leading to the trail. We couldn't find them.

We biked around some more, up and down a few hills, into a neighborhood, then back up those same hills. We were not finding the trail and were wasting daylight. We headed back for downtown and then just kept pedaling.

Out of the corner of my eye I spotted a biker heading the direction I believed we were supposed to go.

"Rhino, follow that guy," I said, feverishly pointing at the man.

By the time we were within a decent proximity of him, we encountered a pole that had locations and arrows pointing every direction.

"Damn. Which one do you think, bro?" I asked.

Rhino looked around and didn't know either. "I'm going to guess that one," pointing to the left.

We went left but soon had to turn around when we came up on a massive body of water.

"Damn, Rhino. Did you even look at your phone?"

"Did you?"

Enough was enough. Rhino snatched his phone from his jacket and this time more meticulously mapped out a route. We began going down a busy road, which brought us right back to the junction of the highway we had already passed.

"Rhino, I thought we were heading toward the trail."

"We are. My phone has us a mile away. Fuck, just trust me."

Everything that happened the night before and then into today had a detrimental carryover effect into our ride. I couldn't stand another minute around Rhino. It was clear that he was running on fumes and wasn't thrilled about how much riding we had left. Yet there was nothing I could do. I couldn't help the fact that he was hungover the previous day and rode like shit. I couldn't help that my brake pad came loose. I needed more from him. I needed to see the mental resiliency that I had seen so often from him. Maybe now the miles were finally starting to break him.

"I'm going to go into the gas station and ask for directions," Rhino said.

"Why? Your phone says to keep going this way and we will run into the trail."

"Yeah, but I want someone else to confirm it."

"So you're going to go inside and waste time talking to some random person. How the fuck do you even know that person will have any clue?" Rhino stormed away without answering. "Fuck you!" I yelled once he opened the door to the gas station.

We had now lost all our connectedness. For as much as I didn't want to be around him, I imagined his disdain for me was worse.

Rhino came out after five minutes. "Yeah, we are going the right direction."

"We already were. You didn't have to go inside to figure that out."

"Shut the fuck up."

"Bro, what is your problem today? You're acting like a dick."

"And you're not helping."

I laughed in disbelief. "Dude, you got problems. I haven't even done anything to you."

"If you're going to keep this up, I'm going to just call my dad and have him bring me to Pine River."

"And cut our whole day short? Wow. Real classy, Rhino."

This was a crossroads for us. I had never fought this hard with Rhino. Neither of us meant to inflict any harm, but we were running out of energy and patience. The trip could have been over for either of us, and we wouldn't have cared. Neither of us realized that if we quit, we would only be cheating ourselves. No one cared anymore about this trip. Our Facebook popularity had decreased drastically. We were riding only for ourselves, and this reality might have brought the both of us down, albeit at different marks of the journey.

Soon I relented and followed him, hoping that his phone would actually bring us to the trail. We went along another busy road and then veered left onto a deserted road.

"We are only half a mile away," Rhino said.

After the half mile, an entrance to the trail appeared and signage indicated it was heading toward Walker. Things seemed for the moment to turn around as we entered the trail. I hooked a sharp right turn, then out of a side yard, a massive German Shepherd bolted my direction. Rhino was about fifteen feet ahead, leaving me exposed to whatever this dog was going to do. Based off my pace and the fact I had to ride uphill, this dog was undoubtedly going to catch me.

I didn't have my legs under me and I feared the worst. I was waiting for the dog's owner to call out after him, but it never happened. I reached for my water bottle, planning to throw it at the dog's face when it leapt at me. I looked back and the dog was now only ten feet away and closing like I was going to be its first meal in three weeks.

I still couldn't muster up any momentum and saw Rhino pedaling hard, but only enough to stay in front of me and away from the dog. We were now past the property of the dog, and I hoped that would save me, considering most dogs know their boundaries and don't challenge them. This didn't happen. The German Shepherd was now at my side, and I prepared for it to bite down into my leg or foot. I took one longer stride and turned with my water bottle, but then the dog was gone. It had backed off and was no longer in pursuit.

I caught up with Rhino and we laughed at the close call.

"I'm just glad I was in front of you, otherwise I might have only one leg right now," he said.

I don't know if he would have tried to save me had the dog grabbed hold of my leg or arm. To be honest, I don't think I would have tried to save him either.

After my freshman year of college, I was at my friend Jesse's house watching hockey. His brother came in and said he wanted to play video games, but Jesse told him no. With Jesse being the older brother, I thought that was the end of it. His brother had other ideas. The two argued back and forth about privileges, who was there first, and everything else you would expect in a sibling rivalry.

After a tense moment, his brother, whose arm was in a cast, preceded to bash Jesse over the head a few times, causing Jesse to bleed.

"Q, help me," Jesse called out, but I just sat frozen in fear. I thought they were joking, but once Jesse's head got bashed around like bowling pins, I knew there was something more taking place.

To this day, Jesse asks me why I merely watched instead of helping.

"Bro, I was simply stuck in time. I literally could not move," is what I always tell him.

The same could be said for this situation with the German Shepherd. Only this time, it did not come to such bloody terms.

We began our trek toward Walker, which was still a marked distance away from Pine River. It was a grind in every sense of the word. We took repeated breaks, desperately trying to keep our muscles loose and agile, but nothing seemed to work. Every stretch would lead to a few minutes of relief, then unbearable pain.

I kept seeing signs with numbers next to the name Walker. I assumed they were mile markers, but they unpredictably changed at every sign. Since they were out of sequence, we had no idea how far it was until Walker.

Eventually, there was a sign on the road that indicated Walker was ten miles away. That meant that we had gone between twenty and thirty miles. It was a pretty pathetic day, from a mileage standpoint. We had breezed through yesterday, but today was another day that was not going in our favor. It wasn't that the wind was unforgivingly gusty. Rather, we just could never find a rhythm. Whenever we seemed to have a pace, one of us needed a stretch break. In addition to the physical ailments, debris was piled up at various points along the trail. Sleet, ice, and snow all derailed our progress. Twice, we had to walk our bikes to a clear point. We simply had nothing going for us. All the previous events had set us back, and we never made a recovery. This wasn't how we imagined our first time on the Paul Bunyan Trail going.

Mercifully, Walker finally arrived. We got off the rigorous trail and took the main highway into the heart of the city. We stopped at Subway for a meal, with the clock next to the cash register now reading 5:12 p.m.

We ate in relative silence, and then Rhino shared his thoughts.

"Bro, let's just call it a day here."

He felt it would be better to end the day here, recuperate, and then get after it tomorrow.

Initially, I took the same stance he did on our first day in Brainerd. "Why would we cut our day short when we have daylight left?" I asked.

"Dude, I hear you there, but let's be real. Let's get a hotel in Brainerd. That way we can guarantee we will get home tomorrow." I listened without talking. "Besides, I know your body is beat up. Mine is too. Let's just cut our losses and try to get home in one piece."

I didn't want to be the one to say it, but I was in the same position as him. I was beat. My body was drained. Getting a ride to Brainerd would have only been a better idea if I had come up with it. I took this acquiescence of miles to mean that the trip had taken us both for all we had. Getting to St. Cloud from Brainerd would be easy.

"Let's just ride down Highway 10 the whole time," I said. "There is no reason to mess around with those back roads."

Bruce arrived and parked his car outside. We began to load the bikes in the back for the last time. The ride to Brainerd consisted of listening to Bruce's heroics from his biking days, and a roundabout way of congratulating us for what we had done. He spoke of his days biking in Wisconsin, which as mentioned consisted of biking to and from work every day, totaling near forty miles.

"There was this hill, and let me tell you. It was two miles high. Going up that thing every single day was a pain in my ass," Bruce said.

It was at this moment that I realized for Bruce this trip had been as much about him as it was about us. Sure, he wanted his son and I to do well, but he also could live vicariously through us in a way he might never have predicted. Bruce left an imprint on me as well. He was a saucy old man, intent on sharing his opinion even if the situation didn't allow for it.

I didn't know what to make of Bruce when I first met him. Rhino and I, like many, didn't really talk about our dads. We loved our dads, but perhaps subconsciously we all compete with our fathers to see how great of men we can become. We need a baseline for our successes and failures, so we seek out our fathers for stories and advice, just to shed light on what we might be able to expect in the future. Because of this, Rhino then elevated himself into his dad's company, surpassing his accomplishments while conjunctively paying homage to a man he holds in such high regard.

For myself, it was similar. My dad was never a long-distance rider, but he was always working and tinkering on bicycles. Ironically, that part never was ingrained in me. We always would go on short rides around the neighborhood, and then as I aged, we extended our treks out to the Coon Rapids dam. At the time, I only went with because it meant we could stop somewhere along the way for an ice cream cone. As I became a teenager, my motivation for going was still the same.

My dad also taught me how to be a man, and not the type of man I was acting like. My dad taught me the importance of being a responsible person, like showing up to school on time, treating people with respect, and being generous toward others.

It's sad, but I wasn't behaving like I should have been. I definitely wasn't responsible, having conquests with any attractive woman who would look twice at me. I spent what little money I had on stupid things. If I ever did spend money on other people, it was only at the bar with an asterisk attached to it. One year I became so self-centered that I didn't buy anyone in my family Christmas gifts. I painfully had to open a gift from everyone else, and then make up a lame excuse for why I had nothing to give back. I had to change and be a better man, but I didn't, and it was ruining my life.

As I look back on it now, whether he knew it or not, my dad was molding the foundation for my future in bicycle riding. On this trip, there was no ice cream, but it certainly was a treat.

I picked back up the love for riding through Rhino. This fact doesn't diminish what my dad, brothers, and sometimes even my mom would do, but Rhino awakened a passion in me I never knew I had. It's similar to being in a rut, and then you meet someone who alters the whole course of your life, like what Nicole did for me.

Rhino gave bike riding a purpose. He will never truly understand just how much it meant for me to have someone like him who I can whimsically call and know that he will be down to go for an adventure. For this, my debt to him is lifelong and unquantifiable.

We pulled into Brainerd on this Saturday night with a quietness that was new to our trio. There were no fireworks at the Super 8, only Rhino and I receiving complimentary but day-old chocolate chip cookies. Rhino left to go buy some alcohol and I sat in our hotel room trying to enjoy the moment. This was the last night of the greatest trip of our lives.

I expected it to be more grandiose than it was. I turned on the television and watched more college basketball. Everything started to weigh on me, psychologically. What was life going to be like when we got back? Would I be able to return to a normal, structured life? Was Nicole still going to like me? I had to calm myself and tune out the negative energy. There was no use in dwelling on the unknown. In life, if you do the right things, generally good things will happen.

Rhino returned with a twelve pack of REDD's Apple Ale. I managed to drink half of one before the taste of rotten apples was too much. BG, our buddy from Rhino's hometown, called and wished us luck on the final day.

At this point I figured that the car ride to Brainerd was my unofficial way of saying good-bye to Bruce. It's always hard to say thank-you to someone who has given so much without asking for anything in return. Bruce saved our trip. We needed his aid to make it all the way to the border. Without him, we might still be dragging our way back to St. Cloud. I knew I was going to see him in the morning, but I wouldn't be able to articulate my gratitude then. To a man, Bruce knew what he had done for us. Rhino and I were too bashful to admit it, and he knew that. Bruce just wanted to be a part of things, and he was, in ways that could never be equaled.

CHAPTER SIXTEEN

The next morning, we awoke to the sound of a screeching vacuum in the other room. The Super 8 definitely didn't waste any time preparing for the next day. We packed most of our things into Bruce's car so that our last ride of the trip would be as easy as possible. Not that we expected anything less, but Bruce was kind enough to bring all our remaining clothes and equipment back to our house in St. Cloud. There were no tearful good-byes to Bruce.

"Thank you for everything," I said while shaking his hand.

"So you remember where our house is? Call me when you get there." Rhino said.

And with that Bruce was gone. Sixty-five miles now stood between our final destination and us. It took two miles to get out of the commercialized section of Brainerd and onto the last stretch down Highways 371 and 10. It was a pleasant two miles and I thought we might just cruise home.

As if the biking gods had a grudge on us, as soon as we got out of the city, major winds were directly in our faces. I wanted to cry because this monster wind was against us over a week ago.

We forged ahead for ten miles before we had to take a break. Those ten miles consumed most of our energy and now we were already into our reserves.

"What do you mean you can't find it?" Rhino asked his dad, who was already in St. Cloud. "Wait. Wait. Who are you talking to? Don't you see my car? Dad, give whoever that is the phone."

I relished the break, taking a few photos to post one last time to Facebook. A man in a beat-up sedan stopped at a stop sign while he waited to merge onto the highway. He tipped his cap and continued on.

Time passed, lunch hour approached, and we agreed on stopping in Little Falls, which was about thirty-five miles away from St. Cloud. We dangerously crossed over a double highway where Highways 371 and 10 intersect. I sped past Rhino to get onto the shoulder as quick as possible. Rhino was still in the middle of the highway when cars started approaching.

"Dude, get your ass moving!" I yelled.

Rhino hurriedly made it to the shoulder. "Close call," he chuckled.

We were in Little Falls but still a short distance from the turn off as we continued to battle hills and the vaunted wind. The one benefit was that the weather had considerably warmed, and for the first time all trip, I didn't have to wear a jacket.

We decided to eat at an American Legion over a Mexican restaurant. The place was dead, as you might expect for a Sunday afternoon. The bartender was a bigger woman in her midthirties who had no genuine love for her job.

Rhino ordered a Corona and I bought us a pizza. It was a cash only place, but neither of us had any. This precipitated another confrontation because Rhino's credit card wasn't working and he wanted me to float him forty dollars. I was down to my last eighty dollars, and even though he said he would pay me back the next day, I still didn't want to do it.

"Wow. You're really not going to give me any money?" he asked.

"Bro, I don't have any money. If I give you this, I barely can eat this coming week."

We quietly debated for ten minutes before he turned away, infuriated that he wasn't going to get another beer. I should have given him the money, but I was in a crabby state and didn't have his interests in mind. More than anything, I just wanted to get back home and see Nicole.

We finished the pizza, then quietly left the bar and began our last thirty or so miles back. We had to merge back onto Highway 10, which was made more difficult by the fact that a minivan wouldn't move over far enough to feel comfortable.

Royalton was our next closest city, about fifteen miles away. The cities were becoming more and more familiar, but the excitement was not at par. Since we were on a busy highway, there was nowhere to pull off and rest. We couldn't even talk. It was so loud from all the buzzing that my head started to hurt.

When we entered Royalton, the shoulder narrowed to about a foot, which put us shoulder to shoulder with the traffic. My legs started to shake thinking that a car might accidentally clip my hip or foot. We were that close to danger. The noise and the nerves became too much. I hopped off my bike and began walking it in the grass.

We got off the highway at another gas station and looked at each other. There was nothing to say. I loved Rhino and the only thing left to do was finish. It was going to hurt, but there was a moment waiting for us; just like when we had come back from Alex and my eyes watered and my euphoric demeanor could not be contained.

"We are this close," I finally said to Rhino. "We are this close," now placing the thumb and index finger on my right hand to within a centimeter of each other. "No one can take this away from us."

When we got near Rice, I turned my head around to yell at Rhino.

"Follow me! We are getting off this highway!"

"What? Where?"

"Just trust me!" I screamed.

I had messed up directions before, but I knew this route by heart. It would bring us straight into Rice and right back to where we were months earlier in the dead of the night.

Nostalgia began to set in as I realized we were ending right where we began. We were only fifteen miles from home. These were the same miles Rhino warned me I could get a DUI on. These were the same roads I experienced while being drunk and rejected. It was the same route where I looked out at the motionless Mississippi River. It was the same place where I told myself, "This is what I want to do with my life. This is how I want to live." Goddamn, it was bittersweet.

The sun was bouncing off the river in a beautiful way when we stopped to take a quick break. I took another selfie to announce our arrival on Facebook and embrace the scenery. Yellow, unripe grass littered every lawn. The snow was practically gone, and people were out walking their dogs or riding their bikes.

As I said earlier, it is hard for men to cry. In this moment, I wanted to cry so bad. I wanted people to see how much I had just persevered through. Like the first time I asked a girl out on a date, I was deprived this sensation, either by my male ego or a dehydrated body.

As we slowly trudged the last few miles along the river, we passed another rider. We exchanged glances and he had a funny look on his face. I initially didn't think anything of it until he doubled back and began riding alongside us.

"Hi, I'm—" I had no idea what his name was as soon as he said it. "Are you the two that rode to Winnipeg?"

"Yes, sir. We are on our way back as we speak," I said.

"On these bikes?" he asked rather rudely.

"Yes. Do you have a problem with that?"

"No, no. I just think it would be hard to get far on that type of bike."

"Dude, I'm in college and broke as fuck."

"We know we need better bikes, but we can't right now," Rhino said.

"Fellas, I'm not trying to diminish what you did. Honestly. You guys did great," the man said.

"Thank you," Rhino said begrudgingly. With that, the man said goodbye and rode away.

I turned to Rhino and barked, "Fuck that guy!"

"He had a point about our bikes."

"Duh, but do you think we can afford to go buy another one just like that?" I asked, angered that Rhino might have agreed with the man.

The next thing I saw was a man with ripped legs passing us on his bike. Normally that would piss me off, but I knew there was no way he was coming from where we were.

We made the turn off the Mississippi, right in the heart of Sartell heading toward Sauk Rapids. A four-way stop neared and we blazed through it. The gas station on the left was where I bought Corn Nuts one time. I laughed thinking about how poorly I had eaten the last ten days.

We would be home within forty-five minutes. The nostalgia was beginning to implant itself firmly into my consciousness. As we passed Benton Station, crossed over the Mississippi, and then rode by the hospital; it was all coming full circle. I couldn't believe we were here. It was worth the long months in the gym and going through all the failed relationships to get to this point. I was going to make it. I earned this.

I still have many great years of biking left in me, but taking the road so familiar to us on our way home felt like a completion of my biking indoctrination. It was like an initiation ritual where you go through so much only to come back to the starting point.

After we passed the hospital, the chain on my bike fell off, a sign of the miles traveled and that my bike, just like me, was done with this journey. I sloppily popped the chain back in and there was only one more stop to make before we went home.

We pulled up to Herbergers so I could reenact my Valentine's Day gig and surprise Nicole.

"You have three minutes," Rhino joked.

I reached for the handle and the door was locked. Panic set in when the other handle didn't open either. The third one worked and I made my way inside. Nicole was closing up at the jewelry counter when I saw her.

"Hey, stranger," I interrupted.

Nicole's face sparkled like the turquoise necklace I later gave her. She was so happy to see me. I kissed her and we both laughed to each other. I couldn't believe I was standing in front of such an amazing woman.

"You look like a bank robber," she noted, breaking the silence.

"You mean I look like shit."

Nicole looked back into my eyes the same way she always did when she had been swept off her feet.

"Nicole, Rhino said I have three minutes and I know you're trying to get out of here. You coming over when you get off?"

"See you soon," she said, smiling and going back to her work.

I walked outside, glad to be back in St. Cloud. We coasted the rest of the way home, taking a right on Eighth Street before making a left into our driveway as we had done so many times previously. A few friends had gathered there to meet us.

"I thought there were going to be news trucks waiting for you guys," my friend Jake quipped.

I took a seat on the stairs leading into our house to catch my breath.

"Rhino, you look like a caveman," Scooter joked.

"I haven't shaved in over a week, bro."

"Yeah, but you look like you just came out of the cretaceous period."

Nicole then walked around the corner. Everyone stopped talking to acknowledge her presence.

"Congratulations, Rhino! You guys did so great!" she said.

"Thank you," Rhino replied, too shy to hug the beautiful woman.

"Do you want to go inside, babe?" I asked, which was met with a round of cheers.

"Of course, Q," she answered. She knew me so well.

We walked into my room and I slowly took off all of my clothing. Nicole sat on the bed and watched. I took a sniff of my armpit and was revolted.

"I can go take a shower real quick, if you'd like," I offered while leaning in to kiss Nicole.

When I got closer, she turned away and laughed. "How about you go do that real quick."

It was the fastest shower I ever took in my life, much shorter than the ones I took as a young boy that used up all the hot water.

When I returned, Nicole and I behaved in the most natural way imaginable. After it was over, I looked into Nicole's eyes, then out the window. The sun was still up and the weather was getting warmer. I had it all. Life was just beginning.

AFTERWORD

Many might assume this trip was done for publicity and attention. I want to clarify that this trip was and always will be about two best friends that went out on the journey of a lifetime to find nothing other than a good time. That is what our biking has always been and always will be. No matter how hard I try, it is so difficult to accurately depict how much energy and determination a bike journey of this nature takes. It is a mental, physical, and emotional grind that truly takes over an individual's life. As much as I hated the physical repercussions of this trip, I would do it over in a heartbeat because of the personal growth that came out of it.

I again want to thank Bruce Brandenburg for all his help; Dave DeLand, Kryssy Pease, Tim Parochka, and Doug Lunney for promoting our trip. I want to thank my mother and father for helping me with some of the financial aspects of this trip. I want to thank my girlfriend at the time for texting me every day, encouraging me to push on and hold nothing back. I love you, Beanie. I want to thank my dad for meeting us and touring a foreign country with me. His efforts were much needed as well. I love you. Lastly, I want to thank Ryan "Rhino" Brandenburg for putting up with me for nearly two weeks straight. We were by each other's side for so long I know how many hair follicles he has left. Ryan, it was the trip of a lifetime, and you are one of the best friends a dude could ask for. Love you, brother.

For those that are curious, Rhino and I have since done many trips, albeit not to the extent of this one. The following year, we biked to Willmar, Minnesota, and Madison, South Dakota. In the fall, we biked back to his hometown of Independence, Wisconsin. In the spring of 2017, I am doing a summer long tour with my friend Mason, who is mentioned in this memoir. We will travel from St. Cloud to Mesa, Arizona, beginning in early May.

ABOUT THE AUTHOR

Raised in Minneapolis, Minnesota, Quentin Super graduated high school in 2010. He credits his mother, father, and Uncle Chuck among the most influential people of his youth.

A graduate of St. Cloud State University for both his bachelor (2015) and master (2017) degrees, Super is a man who is "good at five things." Writing and a continuous search for something more are two of them. He claims to be no different than any other twenty-four-year-old male, his interests including: educating himself to become a more well-rounded individual, going to the gym every day to stay in peak biking shape, a night on the town, or a night in playing EA Sports's NHL video game with his boys. He also has a self-acknowledged unhealthy obsession with Grey Goose vodka, and a seemingly endless search for "the one."

Super has been on many long-distance rides besides the one mentioned in this book, including trips to other northern Minnesota destinations, South Dakota, and Wisconsin. In May of 2017, Super will embark on yet another biking journey, this time traversing all the way from Minnesota to Mesa, Arizona, with his good friend Mason. He plans to write another memoir documenting that trip.

CPSIA information can be obtained
at www.ICGtesting.com
Printed in the USA
FFOW02n1933040817
38379FF